PLAYS A
DANGEROUS GAME

The Stig series

*The Stig Plays a
Dangerous Game*

Look out for
The Stig Drives Again
and more . . .

PLAYS A
DANGEROUS GAME

JON CLAYDON & TIM LAWLER

Piccadilly
P R E S S

For Hope and Eve

First published in Great Britain in 2018 by
PICCADILLY PRESS
80–81 Wimpole St, London W1G 9RE
www.piccadillypress.co.uk

The right of Jon Claydon, Tim Lawler and Kanako and Yuzuru to be identified as
authors and illustrators of this work has been asserted by them in accordance with
the Copyright, Designs and Patents Act, 1988

A CIP catalogue record for this book is available from the British Library.

ISBN: 978-1-84812-645-9
also available as an ebook

1

This book is typeset by James Fraser
Printed and bound by Clays Ltd, St Ives Plc

Piccadilly Press is an imprint of Bonnier Zaffre Ltd,
a Bonnier Publishing company
www.bonnierpublishing.com

'A tame racing driver? Be not fooled.
He is no more tame than the weather.'

Excerpt taken from Top-Secret MI5 Report to the PM

REVERSE GEAR

Bunsfold, England

It was late. The air was so still that anyone out walking would be able to hear the faint buzz from the telephone wires. But no one was.

Shattering the silence, the American boy crashed out of the forest on a mountain bike and on to the deserted road. Beside him, a panting dog kept pace.

On his left he saw the speed camera that had once flashed his dad doing thirty-three. Watch out, son, he'd said. It'll be flashing bikes next.

The lights changed. He set off down the hill and passed the camera doing twenty-five, tops. It flashed, twice. That settles it, he thought. It's busted.

He didn't see the camera silently extend and swivel to follow him, like an insect eye on a stalk. Nor did he catch its laser gaze tracking him all the way to the last lights before Bunsfold.

A black van drew up opposite. Dark windows, throbbing exhaust and a ridiculous number plate: '8AD'.

The dog – a scruffy brown mutt, with a jagged white flash on its forehead – took three steps towards the vehicle and growled.

The boy had suspected that the mansion on the hill needed a closer look, and he'd been right. The deadly tech released from the place had somehow turned his parents into zombie screen-heads in twenty-four hours. He had to raise the alarm.

He listened to the van's throbbing exhaust. Wait – that was a V8. Who'd put an engine like that in a *van*?

Them.

The van door opened and a dark silhouette stepped out. Vaguely human, but jeez . . . had to be over seven feet tall. The boy glimpsed two red pinpricks of light where the eyes should have been.

Time to split.

Boy and dog shot across the lights and charged towards town. The black van roared into a perfect 180-degree handbrake turn and thundered after them.

We're in trouble, he thought. This thing can really drive.

He needed cover fast, and the moonless woods were the only option. He made out the dirt path to Bunsfold Park on his left.

Maximum attack now . . . sixth . . . seventh . . . eighth . . . Top gear.

The boy heard a sinister robotic hum getting closer. The black van couldn't follow but the shadowy figure, it seemed, could.

He turned to see the dark silhouette now running noiselessly behind him at the speed of a family hatchback.

The mongrel skidded to a halt and turned, teeth bared, to protect the boy's escape.

'NO! Here, pal!' screamed the boy, still racing. He couldn't

stop now. Whatever was chasing him was evil. He could sense it.

Then . . . the sound he'd most dreaded. An explosion of barking followed by a single, piercing yelp.

No!

Now he was alone. He *had* to get to the river.

The hum was closing in again. He skidded to a halt. *Think!*

The thing emerged from the trees and walked menacingly towards him.

The boy tensed.

WUMPH.

Suddenly a wounded, scruffy mongrel flew out of the undergrowth and knocked the dark figure to the ground.

As the murky shape lay prone, dog and boy took off towards the bridge.

The river was in sight. The exhausted mutt stopped at the water's edge.

'That's it, pal,' gasped the boy. 'You swim it – I'll jump it.'

But the dog wasn't going anywhere. Still determined to protect the boy's escape it turned, limping, to face whatever was in the trees.

The boy sped up and took off like a stuntman, jumping the stream and landing perfectly on his back wheel. Made it!

The dog barked a warning. Too late.

Two metallic tentacles whipped out from nowhere and grabbed on to each handlebar. The hum again, stronger and deeper than before. The dark figure was back.

It towered over the boy. Human? Spectre? Orc? Hard to tell

under that mask. The boy didn't scare easily, but this thing . . .

A stream of data flashed across the black visor. Whatever it was, it knew *everything* about him.

NAME . . . VIRGIL BUSTER MUSTANG . . . BORN . . . SAN DIEGO, CALIFORNIA . . . ARRIVED UK . . . MARCH 7 . . . SCHOOL . . . BUNSFOLD HIGH . . . BLOOD GROUP . . . O RHESUS NEGATIVE . . .

'Listen, T3,' said the boy defiantly, 'people know I'm here. In fact my dad's on his way right now.'

The stream of LEDs replied.

INCORRECT. HE'S . . . BUSY . . . PLAYING . . . A . . . COMPUTER . . . GAME.

The figure reached out a metallic finger, shot something into the boy's neck and continued its investigation.

DISLIKES: HIS SMELLY MATHS TEACHER . . . BITS IN YOGHURT . . . BRITISH PORTIONS. LIKES *FAMILY GUY* DOUBLE BILLS . . . SURFING . . . DOWNHILL RACING

The world was slipping away, but still the data streamed on.

SECRETLY FANCIES . . . PRINCESS LEIA

Wait a minute . . . how could it possibly know about *that?*

'Well, I certainly wouldn't have said "fancies",' said the boy, rather defensively. 'Respects, certainly. Admires, definitely. But . . . look. Cut me some slack. I'm only thirteen . . .'

TWELVE YEARS TEN MONTHS EIGHTEEN DAYS ACTUALLY

'Whatever. Listen, I haven't seen anything. I'll keep my mouth shut. Pinkie promise. Whaddya say? Let me go. I'll disappear quicker than a fart in a fan factory.'

Another beep. It seemed the evil robot had finally found what it was looking for.

DEEPEST FEAR . . . VAMPIRE.

Oh no. Not that.

It had unearthed the one thing that really spooked him. *But how?*

A night fly buzzed around the visor. The dark shape plucked it from the air then held it, wriggling, right in front of the boy. Slowly the screen/visor transformed into a death-white face with hollow eye sockets, purple veins and fangs. It dropped the insect into its mouth and began to chew. The vampire-face leered.

TASTES LIKE CHICKEN.

Another message flashed across the visor. A confusing one.

SO. WHERE . . . IS . . . *THE STIG?*

'No idea,' said the boy. 'Never heard of it. But here's the thing . . .' he stared up at the creature defiantly. 'I wouldn't tell you if I knew.'

THEN BUSTER LA VISTA, BABY.

A flash of light, illuminating the scene for an instant, then blackness. The last thing Buster saw before he passed out was swings and a roundabout.

He'd made it as far as the playground. So close.

Back across the river, the wounded dog looked down on the scene and whimpered softly.

The shadow turned and walked slowly back to finish its night's work.

FIRST GEAR

Three months later

Sam Wheeler knew three things for sure:

1. he was the new boy at the school;
2. his new locker contained a giant locker-shaped haystack;
3. someone was definitely needling him.

He hadn't left his locker full of hay. That morning he'd left it full of books and PE kit. Now someone had stuffed it like a fat old-fashioned armchair.

He needed his locker back. He gathered up a great spiky armful and made his way outside. With his arms loaded he couldn't open the double doors, so he turned round, stuck his bum out and pushed with that instead. It wasn't the most dignified move he'd ever pulled, but, hey, it wasn't as if anyone was looking.

Oh.

He turned to find a crowd of kids pointing and laughing. In the short list of things Sam hated, being pointed and laughed at came pretty near the top.

Some school they'd sent him to. Thanks, parents.

Ignore them, he thought. And, whatever happens, don't turn red.

Too late.

He made his way to an overstuffed black rubbish bin and somehow shoved in most of the hay. Suddenly the buzz of noise from the assembled kids switched itself off. Sam felt a chill in the air.

He heard a deep voice behind him.

'Oi, Four Eyes. You've missed a bit.'

Sure enough, one strand of hay remained on the floor.

It was the last straw.

He turned. Two big kids in identical camouflage jackets now stood a lot nearer than the others: one tall and thin, one shorter but a whole lot wider, with a dark hood up. He recognised them as the lunks that were hanging around the gate glaring at him when his dad had dropped him off.

His mum's last words over breakfast came back to him. 'Whatever you do, don't get into a scrape!'

'Mum, it's the first day. I'm not likely to . . .'

'Only joking!' his mum had beamed. 'That's why we moved here, remember? So you'd be safe from scrapes!'

Sam had been getting into scrapes since he was two, when he'd worked out how to let the handbrake off his pram at the top of Steep Hill and play Scary Plummeting – the first in a series of hill-related mishaps, the last leaving his poor grandfather in hospital.

So Sam's mum thought they should move to somewhere

flatter. His dad was inclined to agree. Well, he was leaning that way. He understood the gravity of the situation; his son was going downhill fast. Coincidentally, the same went for his dad. He was bored, bored, bored with life in the big city. Mrs W felt the same: where had all the fun gone? So when Gramps suggested they move to a sleepy little Surrey town it didn't sound promising.

Gramps was persuasive though.

'Don't be fooled,' he'd said. There was always more happening in Bunsfold than you might think. Most of it under the surface, perhaps, but there all the same. He knew. He'd been there before.

So they took Gramps's word for it, and moved. New school, new start.

And now look. Two hours at school, two bullies. Nice going, new boy.

Sam turned and glared back at his tormentors. The crowd gasped. This should be fun.

He sighed. Okay, let's see what we have here. On the left, a kid so thin he'd have to run around in a shower to get wet, but as tall as a teacher. On the right, a . . . boy? Bear? Wheelie bin? You couldn't tell under that hoody.

Sam had to find their weaknesses. All bullies have a weakness – that's why they become bullies.

He took a deep breath.

'So I'm guessing it was you jokers that stuffed my locker?'

Silence. The kids just looked. Clearly they were going for 'menacing'.

'That was hilarious. Really. You kill me. But joke's over, eh?'

From inside the wide one's hood came the sort of voice you hear in movie trailers for really terrible films.

'Might be. Might not.'

The lunk lumbered forward with all the grace of a newborn hippo on a slippery riverbank, and said, 'The Cruiser Crew does what it feels like. And right now . . . right now . . .'

He seemed to have run out of words. The taller one helped him out.

'And right now we feel like treating you to some of our famous Bunsfold hospitality.'

The Cruiser Crew! Of course Sam had read about PT Cruiser, the reclusive computer games magnate – almost certainly the only billionaire in the whole village. He'd heard he had a kid at the school – but surely it couldn't be one of these meatballs?

'Show him, Spooner,' rumbled the heavy kid, swinging round and accidently banging his lanky mate hard on the elbow.

'Ow!' whined Spooner. 'Right on the bunny phone!'

A couple of kids stifled a giggle.

And there's *his* weakness, right there, thought Sam. Like a clumsy postman, this Spooner kid mixes up his letters under pressure. Means to say 'funny bone', comes out with 'bunny phone', and makes people laugh. And, once they're laughing, they're not scared of you.

He had to think fast. He stared straight back at the tall kid.

'Spooner. You're a smart fella. What are you?'

'I'm a fart smeller,' replied Spooner. 'Gah! That's not fair!'

This time every kid in the playground – clearly terrified of this pair – successfully kept a lid on their laughter.

Tough crowd, thought Sam. He pressed on anyway.

'Chin up, Spooner. You look like you've received a blushing crow.'

Finally, the playground gave in to a major fit of the giggles.

But the laughter stopped as soon as it started.

The wide one broke the silence. 'Better man up, new kid. It's the boss.'

Oh, that's just great, thought Sam. This walking wheelie bin has a *boss*?

He turned to where everyone was staring.

SECOND

**In which Sam Wheeler meets his nemesis,
and a friendly hand is refused**

Over where the playground met the playing field, a figure was resting on the handlebars of a BMX, staring at Sam.

Nobody moved.

Suddenly the figure threw the BMX like a metal rag doll into a 360-degree tail whip, lifted the front end and wheelied across the playground straight at Sam – finally dropping the front tyre about two centimetres from his toes.

He was impressed. That kind of move was rare enough at a championship meet. Who was this guy? He clocked the captain of the Crew.

A camouflage jacket in the same pattern as the two meatheads', but somehow very different. Hoody folded back, revealing a shock of blond hair, cut in a rather feminine style. A low fringe that almost covered the left half of a rather feminine pair of eyes, ringed with lashes long enough to summon up a breeze when blinked.

Blimey, thought Sam. This bloke is rather, um, feminine. Still, each to his own.

The boss finally spoke to the two lunks, in what sounded

suspiciously like the voice of a . . . girl?

'Thank you, Mr Spooner. At ease, Mr Hummer. I'll take it from here.'

Phew, thought Sam. It is, after all, a girl. And he relaxed a little.

Big mistake.

'Nice bike,' he said, trying to sound cool. It was actually an amazing bike, the kind on which a teenage Terminator might turn up from the future, but he guessed that 'cool' might play better this time. Better than 'WOW!!!!' anyway, which was the only other thing he could think to say.

The girl dismounted and prowled around him like a cat. The closer she came, the more details he noticed. Skin as clear as the back of a postage stamp. Teeth that gleamed like a blank diary page. Even the rather cruel lips looked like VIP versions of most people's – though, for all their perfection, they weren't inviting cheery conversation.

Still no one moved or made a sound.

Whoever she is, thought Sam, she's got a hold on the place.

The girl suddenly burst into life, exploding into cheesy Game Show Host mode, complete with fixed smile and imaginary microphone.

'Well, boys and girls, we've certainly found ourselves a contestant with some real "X Factor" here tonight!' She stalked across the playground, staring down every chuckle. 'So all of you who'd like to vote for our new friend with the big mouth, get on those phones right away as the lines are now open!'

More silence.

'And . . . we have a result! So let's find out how many of you voted for our hippie-haired friend.' Now her nose was right up close with Sam's.

'Oh. What a shame. None. Which by an amazing coincidence is exactly how many friends he's going to make at Bunsfold High. Got that, everyone?' She waited. No one spoke. She seemed satisfied.

'Good.'

She nodded at Spooner and the brick outhouse, and in a flash the two bullies were standing over the new boy. And not in a good way.

Sam clenched his fists. He clenched his teeth. He clenched some other stuff too, but you're going to have to use your imagination there. He shut his eyes and . . .

Something felt wrong. He opened one eye – to find himself alone in a semicircle formed by pupils, into which the bullies had magically disappeared.

There was a moustachioed adult standing right behind him. Not one Sam had seen before, but it wasn't hard to guess his role in life.

The teacher spoke in that sarcastic tone that teacher-teachers teach the teachers they teach in Teacher School.

'New boy, I assume.'

Sam nodded.

'I'll take that as a "Yes, sir",' said the teacher. 'I'm Mr Hornet, deputy head. And jokes about my name are *strictly* forbidden, in case you're thinking of any. One or two young comedians tried some a while back, but after what became of them I can assure you no one at Bunsfold High will attempt *that* again.'

'I certainly won't bee trying it, sir,' said Sam's blonde tormentor, emerging from the crowd with a smile – which the teacher met with the most simpering grin Sam had ever seen.

'It's a real hive of activity this morning, Mr Hornet,' she continued. 'Wasp been happening?'

'I was hoping one of you could tell me. Have you any idea why your young friend here was behaving like a cornered ape?'

'Me, sir? No, sir. And he's not my friend, sir. Never met him.'

'And the straw on the floor. You can't tell me more?'

'Very poetic, sir. But alas no.'

The teacher smiled again, this time even more weakly.

'Miss Cruiser, I can't apologise enough. Seems this new troublemaker has much to learn about how we do things at Bunsfold High. Rest assured, I'll have him firmly disciplined.'

So the gang leader was Cruiser Junior. It figured. As did the teacher's shameless sucking up. Helps in life, being a billionaire's daughter.

'Thanks, Mr H,' she said, smiling sweetly at the teacher.

As Sam opened his mouth to protest, the bell went.

Mr Hornet turned to him.

'Detention for you. Tomorrow after school. And if I find you bothering Miss Cruiser again . . .'

For the second time that morning Sam went very red – this

time at the injustice of it all. Cruiser sauntered over.

'See you later, alligator,' she hissed as she passed.

'It's been vile, crocodile,' said Sam under his breath.

Never mind what she looked like: this kid was Trouble.

But right now Sam knew he had bridges to mend, so he caught up with Spooner on the way to class.

'Come on, mate. I was just kidding around. No hard feelings, eh?' and he offered his hand.

Spooner ignored it and glared.

'Forget it, new boy,' he said.

'You and I will *never* free bends.'

**In which we meet an unusually tall Minnie,
a red-faced henchman and some cheese**

By lunchtime Sam felt as heavy as a suitcase full of memories and as flat as a retired piano key.

He thought he'd handled himself okay, but still hardly anyone spoke to him. No surprise there, after the order from the Crew.

Lunch was a friend-free zone; people actually picked up their trays and moved tables away from him, like in some old prison movie where nobody wants to be seen sitting near The Snitch.

Left to pick through his macaroni cheese alone, he decided there is no more lonely feeling than being the new boy at a school where everyone knows each other, but none of them talk to you. Not that they talked to each other all that much. He'd never seen so many kids staring at screens. Walking down a corridor felt like playing Pupil Pinball, as precisely no one was looking where they were – OW! Sam enjoyed zapping a few killer sprouts and zombie otters as much as the next kid, but this was nuts.

One brave pale adolescent at the next table did manage to drag his face up from his console long enough to ask a question.

'Oh, you're the new bloke,' he stuttered, bloodshot eyes blinking in the sunlight. Then he looked around carefully before whispering the only thing he could think of to ask. 'So go on then . . . what's your high score?'

'Er . . . high score at what?'

The scrawny kid blinked some more, looked confused, then, 'Eh? Xenon of course. Duh.'

'Sorry, never heard of it,' said Sam.

He might as well have said he sacrificed a goat before school every morning and made a packed lunch from its insides.

'Not . . . play *Xenon*? Come off it, mate . . . Nah.' The kid trailed off, head shaking in disbelief and eyes blinking harder than ever.

Just then, the human wheelie bin and his venomous-looking beanpole of a mate swaggered into the dining hall, glowering around the room for any hint of absent respect. And as soon as they spotted a kid talking to Sam, they hurtled over like a pair of cartoon bears chasing a steaming pie.

As the pale gamer quickly shuffled off with his console, Spooner sat himself directly opposite Sam while Hummer squeezed right next to him.

They said nothing.

Sam said nothing.

They kept on staring.

Sam kept on saying nothing.

Hummer began cleaning his fingernails. Which, to be fair, was definitely overdue.

Sam finally broke the silence with the only subject he could think might work at Bunsfold High.

'So, lads. What's your high score?'

Yet more silence. Sam stared back at Spooner.

'Yes, yes, all very scary and everything. But now would you please stop staring at me? You're burning a hole in my face.'

At which point Spooner leaned over and stared even harder.

All right, thought Sam to himself. Time to survey the options. He could either (a) get up and walk away, (b) attempt to engage them with friendly banter, or (c) tough it out.

He chose (c).

'All right. Why don't you two meatheads run along and leave me to this rather disappointing macaroni cheese?'

'Oh yeah?' replied Spooner. 'And why should we do that, exactly?'

'Well, first because you're an ass. And secondly . . . actually I don't think I need a secondly.'

The lanky henchman leaned menacingly across the table.

'Think I'll be staying right here for now, thank you,' he whispered menacingly, his nose now almost touching Sam's. 'Fight in your race.'

But this was the moment Sam finally met the first real human being to be found in Bunsfold High.

Striding across from the other side of the dining hall came an unusually tall girl with short mousey hair. Sam had noticed her staring at him, because she was just about the only kid who didn't have their face stuck in a game console.

The tall girl addressed the cartoon bears. 'Hummer. Spooner. Mr Hornet wants to see you in his study. Now.'

The trainee bullies looked bewildered.

'What for?' said Hummer.

'Strangely enough, he didn't take the time to explain,' said the girl.

'Oh! I think I know why!' piped up Sam. 'And it's good news all round.' He paused for a moment. 'He's finally decided to release you both back into the forest.'

The giant apprentice henchmen rose as one. 'All right, new kid. It's time to teach y—'

But once again the tall girl stepped in.

'I'd get a move on if I were you. Hornet was looking decidedly waspish.'

She flashed a rather sudden smile at Hummer, who blushed slightly in response.

The two henchmen shuffled away.

'Blimey. Thanks,' said Sam to the girl. 'Hornet does want to see them, right?'

'Wrong,' she replied, staring hard into his face as if looking for clues. 'But I guessed you could do with a hand.'

'Very kind of you,' said Sam. 'But won't you need a hand when they find out?'

'Don't worry about me,' said the girl. She leaned over to him and whispered, 'I don't scare easily.'

Blimey, thought Sam. His sort of girl. He took a long, hard look at his new friend.

Standard school uniform. Short mousey hair. Regular number of eyelids and earlobes. No other distinguishing features. Apart from her height she seemed designed to feature in the world's most frustrating police witness report. But today normal was exactly what he was looking for, and he liked her plenty already.

'The name's Sam Wheeler. New boy.'

'Mary-Ann Cooper. Girl. So, new boy: what are some of your favourite things?'

'Cars,' said Sam. There was a pause while the girl waited for him to add something else.

'Er . . . that's it?' she said finally.

'Yup,' said Sam.

'Oh, come on,' said the girl. 'There must be something else.'

Sam frowned, clearly thinking very hard. 'Hmm . . . okay. Bikes. Cars. Football. Cars. Chips. Cars. I used to be into giant meat-eating dinosaurs, but these days not so much. What else . . . Did I say cars? And gaming, a bit . . .'

'But you haven't played Xenon yet,' said the girl, more as a statement than a question.

'No, Mary-Ann,' said Sam. 'How did you –'

'Call me Minnie,' she interrupted. 'Everyone does.'

'Minnie Cooper. That's great,' said Sam, beaming. 'What with you being actually quite tall and everything.'

The girl looked at him blankly. Sam kept going.

'My friends call me Wheels.'

Still nothing.

'Short for Wheeler, see.'

'Well, nice going so far, Wheels. With the Three Amigos. You handled them pretty well. But keep a lookout,' she said. 'Hummer and Spooner are one thing . . . but Cabriola Cruiser is a *whole* other tin of spaghetti.'

'Cabriola Cruiser?!' spluttered Sam, sending a shower of macaroni cheese across the table. 'What kind of name is that?'

The tall girl was too busy avoiding macaroni to reply.

'If that name is a joke, I don't get it,' said Sam. 'And if it isn't a joke, I don't get it. And what's a billionaire's daughter doing hanging around with a couple of losers like Spooner and Hummer? Chalk and cheese, isn't it?'

'Not really,' said Minnie. 'They're all wannabe bullies, after all.' She paused. 'So really more cheese and cheese.'

And right then the bell went. At least Sam had made a friend, sort of. But next lesson was – groan – maths. His day was about to get even worse.

FOURTH

**In which we meet a boy with no first name,
Sam stands up for someone and we get
our first whiff of the Walking Trouser Burp**

On the way to the teaching block, Sam looked up at the clock tower. It was topped by a cockerel-shaped weather vane – with something covering the bird's head.

'Wait a minute. Is that cockerel wearing a baseball cap?' he asked.

'LA Dodgers,' said Minnie. 'Put up there by the American boy. No one's figured out how he did it yet.'

'Sounds like a cool kid.'

'Buster Mustang? He was,' said Minnie. And left it at that.

When they finally arrived at the maths classroom, Sam and Minnie sat down two rows from the front. Hardly his preferred location, but the back row had been colonised by his new friends from the Cruiser Crew. A little distance seemed sensible.

As they pulled out their textbooks, a small pale-faced boy with a shock of sticking-up jet-black hair shuffled down the aisle towards them.

Sam had already noticed him in the playground. His face

wasn't stuck in a games console, which set him apart immediately. Instead he'd spent the whole of break time wandering up and down the edge of the playing fields, deep in thought and wearing that confused, slightly wronged expression that adults get whenever their computer screen freezes.

The pint-sized youth spotted Minnie and stopped by her desk, blushing ever so slightly and shifting his weight from foot to foot as if plucking up the courage to speak.

But nothing came out, and he shuffled on to the back of the class.

'Who's that?' asked Sam.

'Oh, that's Harrison,' said Minnie. 'Another new-ish kid. Only been here a term or so. Arrived the same day as your best friend Cabriola Cruiser, but hasn't made quite the same impression.'

'I see,' said Sam. 'What's his first name?'

'No idea,' said Minnie. 'No one's ever asked.'

'Maybe he just has the one,' said Sam.

'Like Megatron?' said Minnie.

'Chewbacca.'

'Rumpelstiltskin.'

'Yes, that's probably it,' said Sam. Then, with a hint of a smile, 'I think little Rumple likes you.'

'Well, he's only human,' replied Minnie, with no hint of a smile back. 'And not the sharpest pencil in the box. Last term he managed to score the lowest marks in every single exam. Even got a "zero" in maths.'

'Don't you get a mark just for spelling your name right at the top of the paper?' said Sam.

'Not if you refuse to put your first name and just write "Harrison".'

They stifled a giggle. Minnie went on. 'He's a bit weird. Someone said they saw him near the old air base the other night, pushing a giant vacuum cleaner and a pile of stuffed animals in a wheelbarrow.'

Sam just opened his mouth and closed it again. There wasn't a lot he could say to that. But, being new himself and not exactly fighting off friendship applications, he couldn't help feeling for the kid.

'No mates at all?'

'Not in school. Used to see the American boy outside a bit, I think. But when Buster Mustang disappeared Harrison sort of clammed up.'

Just then the classroom door slammed shut and Sam 'Wheels' Wheeler first clapped eyes on the latest – and, perhaps, greatest – in a seemingly endless line of Bunsfold High bullies.

The monstrous – and pungent – Mr Rodius. Ugly, bad-tempered and blighted by a serious personal-emissions problem. Rumour had it that at the last staff party he'd got a bit drunk and made a heartbreakingly enthusiastic attempt to fart the entire theme tune to *Doctor Who*.

Today was geometry, and Rodius worked every angle to make the new boy feel several degrees smaller. He poked fun at his hair. Made snide remarks about his name. And it wasn't just

Sam that got it in the neck. Kids were summoned to their feet, publicly humiliated, then sat back down like sacks.

This isn't teaching, thought Sam. This is classroom whack-a-mole.

But there was *one* exception to Rodius's victim list.

For the duration of the class, Cabriola Cruiser reclined in the back row, breathing unpolluted air through a face mask attached to a tan leather oxygen tank. And each time the odious Rodius addressed her he would bow repeatedly like a nodding dog, grin a creepy smile and wring his hands as if trying to rub away a layer of skin.

And once again it occurred to Sam that it helps in life, being a billionaire's daughter.

Finally the time came for the human whoopee cushion's other speciality. The Just-when-you-thought-the-lesson-was-over Test.

'Right!' he shrieked. 'We will finish today with individual questions *specifically tailored* to expose your true level of mathematical ignorance. And your answers will decide your term grade!'

The entire classroom groaned as one, drawing a distressingly bubbly riposte from the darkest recesses of the teacher's bottom.

'While awaiting your turn, each of you will attend to improving your Xenon high scores. Consoles out, thumbs at the ready!'

Hang on, thought Sam – computer games? In a maths lesson? No wonder this place didn't add up.

'Mr Wheeler!' shouted Rodius. 'Pay attention.' He took a deep breath.

'If n squared minus n minus ninety equals zero, and n to the power of y is an integer, find the negative root of . . .'

Unfortunately Sam tuned out around about the time Rodius said 'n', when he'd begun to daydream about the comparative exhaust roars of a LaFerrari and a McLaren P1.

The tyrannical teacher's question meandered on for what seemed about an hour, finally concluding with a triumphant '. . . What, therefore, is the only prime number to represent x times c squared over y cubed?'

Sam rubbed his chin thoughtfully. 'Hmm. I think the answer would have to be . . . two!' he said hopefully, as this was the only prime number he knew.

'WRONG! WRONG! WRONG!' yelled Rodius, his cry a curious combination of anger and triumph. 'C-MINUS!'

Not for the first time that day, Sam felt himself going very red. He opened his mouth to speak, but Rodius went on.

'And now, um, Miss Cruiser. If I may be so bold to suggest a mathematical problem for you?'

'Yes, yes, get it over with.'

'Thank you, thank you, thank you. Now . . .'

And he paused.

'If there are ten green bottles standing on the wall . . .'

He paused again.

'And one green bottle should accidentally fall . . .'

Again, a pause – to make sure she was following every

word of this complex mystery.

'Then how many green bottles are there *now* left standing on the wall? Take your time.'

'Nine,' said Cabriola, still looking bored.

'CORRECT!' called Rodius ecstatically. 'And a quietly impressive A-star for you! A mathematician of some promise, I'm bound to say . . .'

At which point, Minnie Cooper jumped to her full and considerable height and yelled out, 'Oh that's just RIDICULOUS.'

Silence.

Rodius looked ready to spontaneously combust.

Then, to everyone's surprise, the short kid known exclusively as 'Harrison' got to his feet and uttered the first words anyone at Bunsfold High had ever heard from him.

'Um. What I think Miss Cooper was trying to say, sir, was, that . . . perhaps . . . the question . . .'

But sadly at this point words deserted him.

Rodius was now about to catch fire.

'If you are for ONE SECOND suggesting . . .' He flew down the aisle towards Harrison, crop-dusting the entire row with another merciless bottom bleat as he went.

'Harrison! STAND OUTSIDE THE HEADMASTER'S OFFICE! MONDAY MORNING, FIRST THING! And you, Miss Cooper!'

Sam thought he too had to say something. 'Sir, it really isn't Minnie's fault. She was only –'

'YOU TOO, NEW BOY!'

Enough was enough.

'Yes, sir,' said Sam, *just* managing to keep his temper. 'I'll go and see the Head. I'll tell him how his school is being taken over by a stupid game that's even allowed in lessons.'

By this point every kid in the class was staring straight at him. Blinking like strobes, sure, but still pretty menacing.

'And I'll tell him I think it should be banned.'

There was a gasp of horror from the class, and an audible gusset-gust from Mr R.

Now the whole class – except Minnie and Harrison – stood up as one and inched closer to Sam.

Sam didn't scare easily. But he was scared now. This was like a zombie movie. As the pack edged nearer, the bell went. They backed off.

For now.

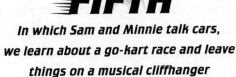

FIFTH

**In which Sam and Minnie talk cars,
we learn about a go-kart race and leave
things on a musical cliffhanger**

The rest of Sam's first day went just about okay. No trouble with the bullies, no more stray hay, but no more real friends either.

He decided to walk home through town. After a day like that he definitely deserved at least a Cornetto. Maybe even a bag of sherbet lemons. Maybe both. He was *that* down.

Bunsfold wasn't exactly a teeming metropolis. For one thing, it was completely surrounded by a thick oak forest, with just one road going through, and a single railway line. It felt isolated, and strangely antique.

Sam reckoned that if his granddad's treasured Hornby train set came with a whole miniature town, instead of just a station, it would probably look like Bunsfold. Stone church with higgledy gravestones, a newsagent, a toy shop, a butcher with strings of sausages hanging up, a sandy recreation ground with goalposts, a murky stream with some swans gliding slightly nervously between the tin cans and upside-down rusty prams. And after 10 p.m. the whole place would be like a ghost town, as if Gramps had put it all back in the loft for the night.

A few large houses lined the hill that led away from the centre, but one stood out. It glowered over the town like the sort of abandoned asylum where someone woulda gotten away with it too, if not for some pesky kids.

Not everything was old-fashioned. There was a speed camera, for one thing. And rather a lot of people on screens. At the bus stop, everyone was looking down, rather than at each other. The whole place gave off a sense of calm concentration that at four in the afternoon wasn't exactly eerie, but wasn't quite normal either.

At home, Sam put on a brave face. No mention of the Crew, the detention or the looming appointment with the Head. Feedback to his parents was on a strictly need-to-know basis. His maths teacher smelled like Bigfoot's boxers; a couple of the kids seemed nice enough. And, yes, at least one was a girl.

They both seemed distracted anyway, like everyone else in this crazy town. Sam grimaced as he remembered hearing that his parents were joining a research group for a new computer game, aimed at adults as well as kids. Bit of extra cash, the chance to meet new friends. They'd jumped at it. The trial had started at midday and already they couldn't put it down. Xenon. Sam felt slightly nauseous.

In the space of an afternoon, it seemed Xenon had turned his mum into a teenager, always on a screen. Dad came in from work glued to his phone, looked up to blink a quick 'Hi, son' and went straight back down again.

At suppertime both parents were still at it. Dad was hopping from foot to foot, so making it as far as the toilet seemed out of the question. Mum managed three words: 'Xenon. Sorry. Pizza,' and carried right on tapping.

So Sam ordered pizza. It took ages to come. The delivery kid didn't look up from his phone either, just shoved the box in Sam's direction and grunted.

My favourite, thought Sam as he looked inside. American Cold.

What a town.

Thanks, parents.

The next school day passed without incident, and when detention came round it wasn't exactly hard labour. Mr Hornet plonked Sam in a room and went off to supervise football practice, leaving him to 'think about his actions'. As he didn't have much of a clue why he was there, there wasn't a lot to think about. So he was delighted when the door opened to reveal a familiar face.

'Minnie!' he said. 'You in detention too?'

'Nope. Just thought you might like some company. Buzz Lightyear has a habit of leaving people in solitary confinement.'

Sam caught on.

'Yes, Mr Hornet has indeed buzzed off. To the playing fields and beyond!'

'Nice,' said Minnie. 'So, if you like cars so much, what's your coolest? Present company excepted.'

'Ferrari 250 GTO,' said Sam without hesitation.

'Interesting. Your worst?'

'Pretty much any family runaround with a horrible soft-top version,' he replied – which reminded him of what was really on his mind. 'So what's the story with my new best friend Cabriola Cruiser?' he asked.

'Oh, just your regular riches-to-riches story,' sighed Minnie. 'Dangerous. Unstable. Power-crazed. She's seriously quick in a go-kart though. Would have won the Champions Trophy first time out if Chief Engineer Simon Spooner hadn't struggled to sort a ridiculously simple electrical problem.'

'What was it?' asked Sam.

'Bat flattery,' said Minnie solemnly.

Sam chuckled, but only for an instant.

'And what about her mysterious dad? I'm guessing that's his huge mansion up on the hill?'

'Ah yes, the Mansion On The Hill. Or MOTH, as we call it for short. Home to PT Cruiser, probably the only billionaire in the whole village. He's only been up there since December, but since he decided to make a Christmas present of himself to Bunsfold, nothing's been quite the same around here.'

The more Sam heard, the less he liked.

'So. Any other kids to watch out for at Bunsfold High School? Or are they ALL total screen-heads?'

'Pretty much,' said Minnie. 'They should rename it Bunsfold High Score.'

'What about the American kid you mentioned?' asked Sam.

'Oh, now *he* was a special case,' said Minnie. 'And . . .' She held up a finger for quiet. A few seconds later Sam heard footsteps coming down the corridor. 'Incoming,' she said. 'Later.'

She slipped out.

A few seconds later Mr Hornet threw open the door, blew hard on his whistle and barked, 'Right, Wheeler, that'll do for today. You don't seem like a bad lad: just a little short on manners where Miss Cruiser is concerned. It would be sad indeed if her father were to reconsider his *very* generous ways. So if I were you I'd set about improving your attitude. Get yourself a hobby! A lot of the children seem keen on this Xenon computer game. Invented right here in Bunsfold, you know. Look into it. And get that hair cut while you're about it.'

'If it's all the same to you, sir, I think I'll –'

'Then there's the Bunsfold TT of course. Weekend after next. Ever tried a go-kart?'

'Bunsfold TT, sir?' asked Sam.

'Latest bright idea of our resident billionaire genius. He's stumped up a healthy sum to turn the town into a racetrack for a day. Big prize money, open to all comers. They'll be coming from everywhere. Foreign TV crews, cheerleaders, the lot. It'll really put Bunsfold on the map.'

'Wait, Bunsfold's not on the map?'

Instead of ticking him off for being cheeky, Mr Hornet actually answered.

'It wasn't for a while: some kind of hush-hush stuff during

the war, and they erased all reference to the town to put the enemy off the scent. But you can't wipe an entire history. All sorts of things have gone on here over the years. *All* sorts.'

'What *sort* of all sorts, sir?'

'Ancient temples, burial sites, crop circles, talking owls, all the usual stuff – then sightings of a mysterious white-helmeted figure that left strange smells . . . then witch hunts, duckings and the Great Runny Bottoms Outbreak of 1618, all in suspiciously short succession.'

Mr H twiddled his moustache.

'A lot of it's just local legend. But now PT Cruiser is putting it on a bigger map than ever. Which has to be good for house prices. If you're interested, download the race application form and get building.'

And that was detention. Sam could think of worse ways to while away forty-five minutes. As he wandered home, he distracted himself by designing the perfect go-kart in his head, while whistling a jaunty tune.

If he'd known what was waiting for him down by the bridge, he might have chosen something a little more sombre. A funeral march, say.

SIXTH

In which we peek inside 'the Cooler'

Buster Mustang knew one thing for sure.

He wasn't playing.

Not Xenon, for a start. He'd seen what it did to his parents.

'Research group' my butt, thought Buster. First victims, more like. They'd only agreed to test it on the Monday before his capture, and by Tuesday they were hooked. Dog never walked, son never smiled at. So the son had decided to investigate. And three months later here he was: a little less fit, but still unbroken.

Ever since his crazy Cruiser captors had first thrown him into a cell – furnished with nothing but a bed, a games console and a surveillance camera or five – they'd been trying to 'persuade' him into 'just giving it a go'. Giving in, more like. Not this kid's style.

He wasn't playing along with PT Cruiser's desperate attempts to break his spirit. What was it last week? The 'letter from home'. He could still hear the smug dillionaire's voice through the cell intercom.

'Read it, you say? Why, sure. Just as soon as you play Xenon. I took the liberty of opening it, just in case. Seems the clever dog

has died. Sorry to be the one to break the news.'

Buster said nothing. He wouldn't give this lunatic the satisfaction of sounding upset.

He hit the REPLY button.

'Copy that,' he said simply.

There was a long pause on the other end of the line. Then . . .

'Copy what?'

Then the vague sound of the voice on the other end talking to someone. 'Maurice . . . what's he asking me to copy?'

Buster lay back down and stared at the ceiling. No way. If anything had really happened to TG, he would have felt it. A howl in the night. A disturbance in the Force.

He missed his dog. But he knew one thing for sure. If that scrappy mutt he'd rescued as a stray puppy in São Paulo had made it to safety that night, she'd come and find him. Or die trying.

He fought back a tear. How long was it now?

He counted the seven-bar gates he'd scratched on the wall with his thumbnail. Months.

Buster clenched his jaw. If they were trying to mess with his head, they'd picked the wrong marine.

'I'd have expected less resistance,' gloated the voice again, 'judging by how limply your father fell in line. As for your wonderful mother, it was as if she *wanted* to be enslaved.'

That line again. The first few times he'd yelled at the creep to leave his mom the hell out of this. It was bad enough feeling like an orphan, without someone rubbing it in. But he'd worked out that the way to stay on top was to stay calm. They hated that.

He reached round to the back of his waistband and retrieved his trusty baseball mitt. On cue, the red-eyed remote camera so un-subtly hidden above the washbasin swivelled round.

Still want to watch me play? Okay, try this.

He sat with his back to one wall and made a perfect pitch at the one opposite. He judged the return path and raised the mitt to catch it perfectly.

Thump, bounce, thud. Thump, bounce, thud. Thump, bounce, thud.

Later that night, the intercom woke him.

'Do you know where you are, Mr Mustang?'

No, where am I?

'You're at the place where secrets go to die . . .'

Then silence.

SEVENTH

In which Sam witnesses peculiar behaviour from a short classmate, and is ambushed on the way home

Sam decided to walk home through the fields. It was a nice day, still pretty light, and the most direct route. What could possibly go wrong in a field?

He'd got as far as the towpath when he spotted the small, scruffy silhouette of the Harrison kid riding a sit-up-and-beg bicycle with a home-made trailer. In the trailer were . . . an old pilot's seat from a fighter jet? And . . . a stuffed wombat? Couldn't be.

Sam decided to follow him and find out what was up.

He trotted along behind at a safe distance, which wasn't hard. Sam reckoned he'd seen faster-moving bollards.

Harrison stopped right next to an overstuffed black rubbish bin. He climbed off the bike, glanced left and right and then started carefully . . . *pulling the rubbish out!*

Sam couldn't believe what he was seeing. What a slob! There was litter all over the place.

Still looking around, the kid then picked up the wombat from the trailer and rammed it into the bin, blocking it completely. Finally, after a lame attempt to put the other debris back on top, he hopped on his bike and cycled away.

Sam was perplexed. There was something a bit weird about this fruit-loop. He hurtled after him, down to where the footpath crossed a stream at a narrow bridge.

Bike and trailer rolled over the bridge – eventually – and disappeared into the trees beyond. But just as Sam reached the middle, the evening took another twist.

Simon Spooner appeared from the trees on the far bank and blocked the way.

Sam considered making a run for it through the stream. But as he looked down to judge the height of the jump, the hooded wheelie bin appeared from beneath the bridge like the troll in *The Three Billy Goats Gruff.*

This was a proper scrape. No teachers, no CCTV, no cops.

Then, from above him, a familiar voice. Calm, quiet and sinister, as always.

Cabriola Cruiser was sitting on a branch over the bridge, one leg hanging down like a leopard's tail.

'That's right, new boy. It's us. Your friendly neighbourhood Cruiser Crew. And here you are, all on your lonesome. Now, seeing as you enjoyed maths so much today, here's a problem for you. Two big versus one little: what are the odds? Easy for a smart lad like you. You hardly need lessons at all. Except, perhaps, in . . . manners.'

Yeah, yeah, yeah, thought Sam to himself as Spooner and Hummer lumbered towards him. Let's get on with it.

'You're going for a little dip now, new kid,' drawled Cabriola. 'I hope you're good at holding your breath, because you're about to encounter my good friend Mr Hummer, the Human Ducking Stool.'

The walking SUV lumbered closer. But just as Sam began to shiver in anticipation of a proper soaking, something strange began to happen.

Softly at first, then quicker, a gentle breeze blew in from off the water. The wind washed droplets over Sam's face, carrying the hint of a faraway lullaby played on rusty bagpipes. A murder of crows rose startled from the ground and wheeled away in formation.

Sam realised that Cruiser wasn't looking at him at all. She was looking out over him and across the field, and the colour had drained from her face.

Spooner's courage had clearly failed him. He loped into the woods yelling, 'EVERYBODY WON ARRAY.'

Hummer clumped off through the water like a dizzy toddler after a whole pack of wine gums.

Sam didn't want to turn and look.

But he turned and looked all the same.

On the other side of the field he could just make out a lone figure standing in the gloom.

Its arms were crossed and it stood with legs apart. And it was staring, silently, straight at Cabriola. Sam caught a glimpse of . . . a white helmet? He couldn't be sure.

Sam's heart was pounding. He turned back in time to see

Cabriola jump down from the branch, land soundlessly like a cat and melt into the trees.

He whirled round again for a better look at the mysterious figure. But apart from a weird whiff wafting on the wind there was no sign. Sam struggled to identify the smell. Was it . . . wet tarmac? And . . . an exploding cigar?

Whatever it was, he was grateful. Spooked, but grateful.

But who on earth *was* he?

EIGHTH

In which we meet Fish Trousers, Todger's Guff and Gramps, and one of them starts a remarkable story

Sam Wheeler slept badly that night. He had a crazy dream about vampire bats, and being chased through the forest by something indescribably evil. Cabriola Cruiser was in it too. On a witch's broom.

When he woke up, he wondered where he was – until his carefully assembled model cars came into focus. Chevy Corvette . . . check. Porsche GT3 . . . *jawohl.* Renault Alpine GTA . . . *mais oui.* Then he remembered it was Saturday, and he wouldn't have to go back to that nuthouse of a school for two days.

He gazed at the poster for the film *Senna* on the wall. He'd gone to see it with Gramps, and . . . of course! Gramps was out of hospital today, and coming to live with them. Sam felt excited, but most of all relieved. The accident had all been his fault – and although he'd been forgiven on his first visit to the recovery ward it hadn't stopped him feeling terrible.

Though Gramps was very old, close your eyes and you wouldn't have known it. He was still smart as a whip and up for a laugh. And he didn't scare easily either. He was a legend in Sam's home town for chasing a gang of hoodies out of the shopping mall, armed with just a tin of prunes and a rolled-up copy of *Sporting Zimmer Frame.*

But if you'd flown eighty missions in a Mosquito fighter bomber during World War II, you wouldn't scare easily either.

That afternoon Sam was delighted to find Gramps parked on the sofa watching the horse racing. He made him a cup of tea and a plate of plain chocolate digestives, quietly closed the kitchen door so Mum couldn't hear – not that she'd be interested in anything but Xenon – and sat down on the floor in front of him.

'What's up, little fella?' said Gramps, still staring at the 12.30 from Aintree. 'That's your serious face. Goooooooooo on, Fish Trousers, you little beauty . . .'

Sam would have to compete with the horse racing. But he had to tell somebody.

So it all came out. The bizarre story of his first week in Bunsfold. The Xenon craze. The Cruiser Crew. Minnie Cooper and Something Harrison. The stuffed wombat. The odious Rodius. Everything.

Gramps listened with one ear on the telly. The 12.30 was obviously a *very* long race. Right until Sam got to the mystery man in white.

'. . . and then, out of nowhere, this, this . . . bloke appeared. At least, I think he was a bloke. He was dressed totally in white – even a white helmet – except . . .'

'Except for a dark visor,' Gramps interrupted. He turned to face his grandson, and suddenly Fish Trousers being neck and neck with Todger's Guff didn't seem to matter at all.

Gramps leaned in. 'And he said nothing?'

'Er . . . yes. Just stood there. Gramps . . . you know who it was, don't you?'

His grandfather sat silently for a moment, then said quietly to himself, 'Challenge accepted, old friend.'

'What challenge? Gramps? Are you okay?'

The old man was deep in thought. Eventually he breathed a deep sigh, and continued.

'The story I'm about to tell you, Sam – promise to keep it to yourself. But you, at least, need to hear it.'

Then Gramps Wheeler took a deep breath, sat back and told a tale he hadn't told for over seventy years.

'It was March 1943. My eighth mission, and probably the most dangerous of them all . . .'

REVERSE GEAR 2

A war story

(featuring a mysterious figure in white)

'Gestapo headquarters in Bremen. Night raid, fast and low. Well, we did it, Sam, but we paid a heavy price. Strafed by anti-aircraft fire. Alf bought it, poor bloke, so I was on my own. And I'd taken a bullet straight through the kneecap. On cold days I can still feel some of it in there.'

He shifted in his chair, rearranged his left leg, grimaced and went on. 'I had to get back, but as I banked for home I realised the flak had taken out my instruments. No fuel gauge, no altimeter, no compass. I must have passed out from the pain, and when I came round I'd made it as far as the North Sea. But I was losing altitude fast. I could see the waves right underneath me . . . huge, black and scary as hell. And I had no idea which direction I was flying. For all I knew I was heading straight out to sea, and when the fuel ran out . . . well, life expectancy in the water was about five minutes. Not a good way to go.'

'So . . . what happened?'

'A miracle. I was close to passing out again and the world was beginning to slip away. And then . . . it happened.'

'What?'

'Turns out I had a guardian angel. A Spitfire shot out of nowhere at incredible speed and manoeuvred straight in front of me. Suddenly it banked to port and I realised it was leading me back to base. I'd been flying straight out to sea. If he hadn't turned up, I'd have ended up ditching about twenty miles from land. So I got straight on the radio to thank the pilot. But the strange thing was he didn't make a sound. Not a squeak. The only noise coming out of that plane was . . . music!'

'Music! What kind of music?'

'"Yes! We Have No Bananas" sung by Billy Jones and His Pyjama Bottoms. Then suddenly he was gone. Bang. Diving to port in a big hurry. Sam, I was scared as hell. Just instinct, but I knew something was wrong. And then I knew exactly why he'd disappeared.'

'What was it?'

'Wolf Pack. Three Messerschmitt night fighters, and I was a sitting duck. They came out of nowhere, guns chuntering. God, I hated that noise. Okay, Squadron Leader Wheeler, I thought. Now it's goodnight, Vienna.'

He paused for a moment, and for the first time ever Sam thought he saw him tremble.

'But I was wrong.'

Gramps paused again, closed his eyes then continued.

'Suddenly, hurtling out of the darkness from above came the Spitfire. Flying straight at them in a dive so steep there was no way he could possibly pull out in time. But he did, by God. The Messerschmitts broke formation and went straight after him. And then I witnessed an exhibition of pure flying genius. Those enemy fighters were chasing a shadow. And all I could think was . . . just who the blazes IS this pilot?'

'So what did they do? When they realised they couldn't catch him?' said Sam.

'Something I'd never seen before. They disengaged from combat then slowly flew alongside us . . . saluting. All three of them. I think they were as dazzled as I was. And they recognised a great opponent when they saw one.'

'But as they flew past I saw markings on the leading plane that made my blood run cold. A tiny painting of a slice of moist, dark cake with a glazed cherry on top. The unforgettable mark of Germany's greatest fighter pilot: the Black Forest Baron. Anyway, as soon as they'd gone I was straight on the radio to the Spitfire to thank him.'

'Did he say anything this time?'

'Nope. All I could hear from the cockpit was a "Teach Yourself Eskimo" language lesson. Quite strange, looking back on it. Anyway, when we finally saw lights in the distance, he banked to leave. And then, in the moonlight, I finally saw . . . him.'

Sam felt a chill go down his spine. He knew exactly what was coming next.

'He was dressed in white overalls and a shining white helmet with . . .'

'A dark visor,' whispered Sam.

They looked at each other in silence for a moment.

'I learned more in that hour over the North Sea, Sam, than I've learned ever since. I learned what words like courage and sacrifice really mean. I learned that in a war, camaraderie can exist even between the fiercest opponents. And I learned how to say, "Your parents' igloo is pleasantly warm," in Eskimo.'

'Anyway, I got the Mosquito down somehow. Strangest thing, but the Spitfire had led me right back here, to Bunsfold. It was a top-security air base back then. Some even said it was the headquarters of the mysterious Head of Intelligence.'

'Who was he?' asked Sam.

'No idea. His identity was the most closely guarded secret of the war. The only thing anyone knew about him was his codename: "The Producer". Funny chap. Always wore a white lab coat. He gave Alf and me the instructions for the mission in a white envelope marked YOUR CHALLENGE.'

'Challenge accepted,' remembered Sam. Gramps nodded, and went on.

'The next day I'm recovering in hospital talking to my commanding officer on the phone.

'"Welcome home, old man," he said, "we thought you'd bought it."

'So I told him about the mission, the Spitfire, everything. I said, "I'm sorry, sir, you must think I'm quite mad." But he just paused and told me to stay on the line. When he came back, he said, "I'm patching you through now to the War Room. Please repeat everything you just told me to the prime minister." '

Sam couldn't believe what he was hearing. 'You were

talking to . . . Winston Churchill?'

'The great man himself. So I told him everything and muttered, "I'm sorry, sir, you must think I'm delirious." He was quiet for a moment, then said, "On the contrary, Squadron Leader. I entirely believe you. This is not the first time. We are once again greatly in his debt."

'"Excuse me, sir," I asked, "but who on earth is he? I've simply never seen flying like that."'

Gramps spoke Churchill's words slowly.

'"He appears only in times of great need. Or, it seems, when there's a close race to be won. Wherever evil takes the upper hand, he appears to set things right. Or just appears. We're not entirely sure."

'Then,' said Gramps, 'he said something I'll never, ever forget.'

'What? What did he say?' asked Sam, eyes even wider.

'"Some say he is merely a phantom – a figment of our imaginations. And that he can only get to sleep if there's building work next door. All we know is . . ."'

He paused for a moment.

'"He's called The Stig."'

NINTH

**In which Sam tries to play Xenon,
a clever dog makes another appearance
and birds stop singing**

Sam needed to get out and clear his head, because Gramps's story had it spinning. Seeing as his stupid show-off bike-riding had caused the accident, his usual remedy of a fast off-road cycle was still out of the question. He wandered into town in search of the next best thing – a kickabout.

But he couldn't find any kids to play with. None at the football pitch, no bikes outside the newsagent, no toddlers at the swings. Weird.

He figured he'd buy a ball to kick around himself until someone – anyone – turned up. So he walked into a narrow, shabby shop with faded gold letters above the door reading TOYS-GAMES-SPORTS. He started looking around for the sports section. But all he could see were computer games. Well, one computer game.

'Good morning,' said a quiet voice.

Sam jumped. Behind the counter was a kindly old gentleman trying to remember how to smile. Up from where had *he* popped? Sam held his nerve.

'I'd like to buy a ball, please.'

The old shopkeeper looked at him through a fog of memories, hopped twice from foot to foot as if suddenly remembering he needed a wee, blinked rapidly and gently set a console down on the counter.

Not him as well. At his age?

'Ah yes. I thought I might be seeing you soon. I remember selling your brother his first ball.'

'Um . . . we've only just moved here. And I'm an only child.'

The shopkeeper wasn't listening.

'Ball. Yes. Let me see now. Boy. Wants to buy a ball . . .'

Sam had another try.

'Round object, full of air. Bounces when dropped. Shifts when kicked.'

'You want to buy a ball to *kick*?'

I know what it is, thought Sam. I've wandered into the Royal Society for the Protection of Balls.

The shopkeeper finally came back to the counter, blowing dust and spiders off what he insisted on calling an 'old, *real* football'.

Sam paid and headed for the door, and the old gentleman jumped straight back on to his console. Sam had never seen someone his age playing before.

'What's the game?' he asked, though he already knew the answer.

'Oh. A game beyond all imagining,' answered the shopkeeper, his voice low and respectful.

'Xenon. Of course,' said Sam flatly as he made for the exit.

'Invented right here in Bunsfold,' said the shopkeeper quietly to himself with pride.

Good for Bunsfold, thought Sam, before slipping out to find some real kids to play with.

Back at the football pitch a scruffy brown mongrel – with a jagged white flash on its forehead – was lying in the sunshine by the goalposts, watching Sam intently from a distance. Sam tried calling it over, but the dog stayed exactly where it was.

Finally he spotted some kids his age over by the trees. He strolled over, but his heart sank a little when he realised they too were all looking down at something in their hands. So it wasn't just Bunsfold High kids, parents and old shopkeepers. Naturally they didn't notice him, so he spoke first.

'Fancy a game?'

Not one of them looked up. A wiry kid in a Call of Duty T-shirt at least replied. 'Playing.'

'I mean a real game. In the sunshine.'

'Can't. Glare. Gotta stay in shade.'

'Aw, come on, fellas. I'm new in town. I've got a ball that's just dying to be walloped into –'

Call of Duty looked up and glared, eyelids flapping like a broken indicator.

'Don't you know not to interrupt while someone's playing –'

'Don't tell me,' said Sam. 'Xenon. Blimey. Does anyone round here ever switch Xen-off? How come I've never heard of it?'

'New,' said Call of Duty through gritted teeth. 'Only available in Bunsfold. Until next month at least. Now LET ME PLAY!'

Meanwhile, on the other side of the football pitch, the scruffy hound – who'd been watching everything – suddenly jumped up and started limping towards Sam.

At least someone likes me, thought Sam. As he turned away, one of the other kids, a straggle-haired specimen a little younger than the rest, spoke up.

'Sorry,' he said. 'It's just that it's . . . it's quite a game.'

'What kind is it?' asked Sam. 'FPS, RPG, Driver, Action, Sim . . . ?'

'Oh no,' said Straggly. 'It's much bigger than those. It's the ultimate. It's . . . everything.'

'So,' said Sam, 'mind if I try it, then?'

'All right. Do the Initiation. Only takes a minute. Then get your own, eh?'

'Thanks, mate,' said Sam as the kid passed him his phone.

Sam pressed INITIATE. The machine gave an eerie sound.

BZZZZZZZZeeeeeoooowwwww eeehhhhooooooooo . . .

Then something very strange happened.

The mongrel suddenly pinned back its ears, hurtled full tilt towards them and unleashed the loudest bark Sam had ever heard.

'Blimey! Does that belong to any of you?' asked Sam, passing back the phone and turning to face the mad mutt charging across the pitch.

The kids weren't listening. They were staring over his shoulder.

Not again, thought Sam. Why are people always staring behind me? What am I, a pantomime horse?

But with a sound like that, he really couldn't help checking it out.

Coming towards them, straight over the grass, was a black Mercedes Vito van with darkened windows and oversized tyres.

Holy moly, thought Sam, catching the thunderous rumble of its exhaust.

As soon as the dog saw the van, it spun round, hurtled back across the pitch and made a dash for the open land beyond.

The van gunned its engine and hurtled after the sprinting mutt. Sam watched in horror as it got ever closer. They were going to run it over! At the last minute it swerved alongside the dog and the side door opened. A robotic arm with a huge claw emerged and lifted the animal off the ground, all four legs still running in mid-air like Scooby-Doo.

Sam raced after them, but he needn't have bothered. The mongrel – which looked as if it knew what it was doing – wriggled sideways, twisted downwards and leaped free of the claw.

The van skidded to a halt and reversed towards it. The dog dodged away. Forward went the van, then backwards, then gently to one side then forward again. It looked like an audition for *Strictly Come Vanning*. As the elusive mutt

skipped out of reach yet again, the Merc's back wheels began spinning in the mud.

Calmly, the dog hobbled back towards the woods. As it passed Sam, it paused to stare up at him with two huge, soulful and rather lonely brown eyes.

Sam caught a glimpse of scratches all over the dog's back, and a nametag on its collar.

All it said was 'TG'.

The briefest wag of the tail and it was gone, into the forest and out of sight.

The big black Vito finally hauled itself out of the mud. The claw shot back inside. The monstrous van zoomed into the distance, quad exhausts roaring crossly.

Sam scratched his head. He'd only been after a friendly game of three-and-in. What on earth had he got himself into? And why had the dog barked at him like that? He looked around for some sort of explanation.

There was no sign of the kids. Though if he'd known where to look, there was *something* taking an interest in him.

Sam shivered slightly. In a strange way he didn't quite understand, he could sense something nearby.

Something wicked.

Dark clouds began to roll across the sky like a tarpaulin. Everything fell silent. Even the birds had stopped singing.

Sam could see nothing, and shrugged. But it's hard to spot a tall dark shadow behind a wall of trees if its owner knows exactly how not to be seen.

One of the swings moved back and forth from the force of the van's airstream, creaking slowly in the silence, until it too came to a halt and left the warm summer air as still and quiet as an abandoned pizza box.

TENTH

**In which we learn how little a dillionaire
wears, Cabriola gets frustrated
and so do we, trying to rd hr mssgs**

The reclusive computer games and armaments billionaire PT Cruiser had never bothered to meet his daughter, Cabriola.

He found her 'insufficiently interesting'. And when you've been blessed with the world's only four-figure IQ, you're easily bored.

Besides, he had a lot on. Spiteful drone weapons don't just invent themselves. And dangerously addictive computer games take quite a bit of time to get just right. But once you do, oh boy. It's like owning your own bank.

His Cruiser Missiles and battle drones had been useful money spinners, sure, but this was in a different league – or, as Gamesmaster General PT liked to put it, 'on another level'.

So these days he was less about warring and all about gaming. Hints, tricks, cheats – he knew them all. He'd invented them.

The Cruiser Corporation's first games – Space Inhalers, World of Walmart, Call of Nature – were just research. Even the ones mainly for phones – like Very Cross Sparrows and

Candy's Mush – were merely steps on the path towards his crowning achievement.

Xenon.

Sometimes he thought back to his college days in California. Pretty much all his class were tech billionaires by now. Big deal. PT Cruiser was a dillionaire. That's like a billionaire, but two levels up. And, anyway, he was built for bigger things than obscene wealth. World domination, for a start. Sure, the other guys might get close by accident, but their hearts weren't really in it.

PT was committed. So committed that he'd upped USB sticks, left California and settled here, in a handily sleepy English town he liked to call Silicon Sandpit.

It wasn't just any sleepy English town. His research showed that Bunsfold, Surrey, England, was where The Stig was most likely to appear. PT's white-helmeted nemesis. The Last Great Un-knowable.

So it was here that his evil plans would toddle into life, grow and learn. Today sleepy Bunsfold; soon, the world.

He thought of his old college 'friends' with a silent sneer. Amateurs, all of them.

You never saw any of them in a tie. Their uniform was dressing down: T-shirts, sneakers, jeans.

But PT took *everything* to the next level, and dressing down was no exception. He kept all clothing to a minimum: plain black boxers, plain black hooded onesie. Colour and tailoring were *so* last millennium.

But while not having much on in the wardrobe sense, he had an awful lot in the diary. So he decided that, for now, all communications with his daughter could be managed by 'live chatting' on the Cruiser Corporation's experimental anti-social network, FaceAche. Yes, he could have let Cabriola play Xenon and wormed inside her mind, but PT kept two lists in his head. One was called Things I Want To Know About Everyone. It contained one word: *Everything*. And one called Things I Want To Know About Cabriola. It was mostly empty.

The arrangement suited Cabriola just fine. The last thing she wanted was an embarrassing dad around all the time. How lucky she was.

It was the extravagant public gestures she hated most. Though Cruiser Senior wasn't even distantly concerned with impressing Cabriola, he *did* think it important to keep the locals dazzled.

Like that day she forgot her gym kit and he'd hired Harry Styles to bring it to school. In a helicopter gunship.

Immediately after the incident, Cruiser had been curious. Why had Cabriola's trainers been torn to shreds by a mob of screaming schoolgirls and the pieces kept for mementos?

'So. This Barry Styles. You all like him, yes? I'm thinking of buying him and having him dismantled by the Research Department.'

'He's called Harry, Dad.'

'Okay. Barry Harry. I shall buy him anyway, despite his silly rhyming name.'

'Dad. You can't just *buy* people!'

When her father burst into a full two minutes of helpless laughter at this, she decided he was right. It was indeed best they forged their own paths through life – as he'd spent twelve years telling her. Never having met him, she hadn't missed his company on the flight over from the States: she'd been an unaccompanied minor pretty much from birth. And having an entire wing to herself in each of their seventeen homes had its upsides, like never having to share her bathrooms – and its downsides, like never sharing a sofa. But, on balance, this was WAY preferable.

And so it was that today, yet again, PT found himself stuck in another fortnightly three-minute live-chat catch-up. He was bored already.

Cabriola: Dad. Need 2 update U on some strange events ystrdy.

PT: Nuff with the 'Dad' alrdy. Will this take long?

Cabriola (rolls eyes): Trst me. U want 2 hear.

PT: Hit me.

Cabriola: K. My prtvs dtctd n tttd prblm n th nw by, Sm Whler.

PT: Cabriola. Leaving out the vowels may be vry modrn but it doesn't make it any qickr if I can't figr out WHAT UR TYPING, does it?

Cabriola: Sorry. My operatives detected an attitude problem in the new boy, Sam Wheeler. Bttr?

PT: Mch. Cntinue.

Cabriola: So an uncomfrtble 1st day at Bnsfld was organised and then last night we intercepted him down by Brooklands Brdge.

Cabriola told her father of the ambush by the stream, away from cameras and screens. And how something spooky had happened there.

Cabriola: Evrytng was under control til the apprnce of a creepy dude in a white rcng suit.

Long pause. Then . . .

PT: ??????

Cabriola: Everything was under control until the appearance of some creepy bloke wandering around the forest in a white racing suit.

PT: And a white hlmt. With an impntrble blck vsr.

Cabriola: Impenetrable black visor?

PT: Thts wt I sd.

Cabriola: Ys! U . . . kno him?

Longer pause. Blank screen. This was unusual. Cabriola was a little unnerved. Then, finally:

PT:	Did he leave a smell behind? Of . . . exploding cigar?
Cabriola:	More like . . . an nstck plstr.
PT:	Ah yes. Of course. The unstuck plaster. The sightings begin.
Cabriola:	K, wt am I missing here? Who was it?
PT:	Some say his soul is made of carbon fibre, for added strength and lightness. And that he always knows exactly Where Wally is. All we know . . . Oh never mind. This boy U & yr frnds were 'educating' on the brdge . . . what was his name agn?
Cabriola:	Wheeler. Sam Wheeler.
PT:	Give me a second . . . Hmm. No data. So he's a Resister.
Cabriola:	If you mean hav I seen hm plyng your stpd cmputr game, no. But hes new in town n im not sure NE1 has askd him 2, so . . .
PT:	And he's not just bscally dim, like the short boy Harrison?
Cabriola:	No. Just not as smrt as he thnks.
PT:	Hmm. Okay. Time's up. Leave me to process these new inputs.
Cabriola:	But – wt abt the new go-kart? The race is ONLY 2 WEEKS AWY !!!!!
PT:	Them's the breaks. Leave me to my work. And Cabriola?
Cabriola:	Wot.
PT:	Don't use all the ht wtr.

ELEVENTH

In which we enter the headmaster's
office and hear a grim warning.
More fun than it sounds

Walking to school on Monday morning, Sam stuck to the roads. Not that he was scared or anything.

The surface was still damp from last night's rain and a familiar smell rose to his nose: wet tarmac. He thought of Gramps's story and the white apparition. He'd found it hard to think of much else ever since.

There was no sign of the Crew at the gate. Kids were shuffling in, staring down at their screens with no fear of being tripped up by a Hummer Size 13. If this was the effect of the white weirdo, well, Sam was all for it.

He finally got someone to look up long enough to grunt the way to the headmaster's office. He read the name on the door: B. LEYLAND, HEADMASTER. He turned with a start to see the Harrison kid standing right next to him, in that unnerving way he had of suddenly being just *there*.

Perfect, thought Sam. The ideal opportunity for a few choice words on the subject of stuffed wombats and litter bins.

But he thought better of it. There was an awkward silence.

So Sam blurted out the only other thing he knew about his new companion instead.

'So they tell me you fancy Minnie Cooper.'

Harrison looked cross, and spluttered. And just then the object of his embarrassment sauntered round the corner.

'Hello, boys,' said Minnie. 'Good weekends?'

Both boys instinctively stood a little straighter.

As Sam opened his mouth to say that he'd actually had quite a weird weekend, thanks for asking, the study door opened. The headmaster appeared, looking distracted. He glanced down at the three pupils, sighed and motioned them into his office.

'Right, let's get this nonsense over with. I haven't caught up properly with Mr Rodius, but whatever the reason he's sent you to me just . . . don't do it again. Clear?'

The children all nodded.

'Then let that be an end to it. And I recommend you keep your heads down until this blows over.'

'Yes, sir,' said Minnie, as innocent as could be. 'We'd all dearly like to clear the air with Mr Rodius.'

'Mr Wheeler?'

Sam picked up the theme.

'I'm sure we'd all like to breathe more easily in future maths lessons, sir.'

The headmaster gave him a look, then turned to Harrison. 'Anything to add?'

'I'll . . . keep my nose out of it for now, sir, if that's okay.'

The headmaster sighed again. 'All right, all right. He is a bit on the whiffy side. A staunch Friend of the Sprout, I'm afraid. Some of the staff still can't watch the start of *Doctor Who* without feeling queasy. But the fact is he's an excellent mathematician, and –' he paused, as if reaching for something positive to say – 'and we haven't had a mouse problem since he joined.'

The headmaster gathered up his files and marched the boys towards the door.

'Anyway – enough. Whatever nonsense you've been up to, make this the end of it. And if I get wind of any more . . . um . . . yes, well . . .'

He suddenly turned and stared at the three of them.

'You seem pretty lively for Bunsfold pupils these days. I'd almost forgotten what it felt like having children answer back.' He paused for a moment. Then, 'I've a question for each of you.' And he paused again. 'Have you ever played Xenon?'

Interesting, thought Sam. Let's see where this is going.

None of them saw the overstuffed black wastepaper basket by the desk silently swivel to follow him, a tiny protruding red eye scarcely visible among its contents.

So the three kids just stood there, looking as stumped as Manx cats in a Waggiest Tail competition.

Minnie broke the silence. 'Gaming isn't really my thing, sir,' she said.

'Mr Wheeler?'

'No, sir. Although I must say you're not the first person to ask me that.'

'Mr Harrison?'

'No, sir. I've tried them all. Mine Raider, Tomb Craft, Call of Nature Four. But they're not for me.'

The headmaster was looking serious now, and turned to Sam. Unfortunately Harrison hadn't quite finished, and went on.

'There's also a popular one called Gran's Best Auto, apparently, which is an interesting question. Think I'd have to go with the Nissan Note on that one. Or Honda Jazz, perhaps.'

'And Xenon?'

'Oh no, sir. I wouldn't know where to start.'

The headmaster looked deep in thought. 'Well, I have two requests of you. First, stay away from Xenon.'

'No argument from me,' said Sam. 'I've seen what it can do. Up close. Why not just ban it, sir?'

The headmaster looked at him, hard. Then he said quietly, almost to himself, 'All that is necessary for evil to thrive is that good men do nothing.'

The silence that followed was becoming awkward when Harrison piped up.

'And the second, sir?'

'Hmm?'

'You said two requests.'

'Oh yes. Stay away from the forest at night. I've already lost one boy this year.'

'Blimey. Who, sir?' asked Sam, eyes wide.

'Virgil "Buster" Mustang,' answered the headmaster. 'Came to us from across the pond. Turned out to be the best cyclist around here by a downhill mile. There wasn't much that boy couldn't do on a bike.'

The American boy again. Not just handy at climbing clock towers, thought Sam – also an ace cyclist. Figures. Sam had been pretty handy on a bike himself in his past life. But this wasn't the time or place to tell anyone. When Gramps's accident had happened, he'd made a promise. And he always kept his promises.

The headmaster continued. 'He was last seen one night last spring, riding his bike into the forest. Then . . . well, he just disappeared.'

'Where to?' said Sam.

'That's the thing about disappearing, Mr Wheeler. No one knows.'

The headmaster fell silent for a moment, deep in thought. Then the bell went and he jumped to attention. But before he walked away he turned to the trio one last time, looking deadly serious.

'Be careful out there. Something very dark is loose in Bunsfold. I don't know exactly what quite yet, but I think I'm getting close. Either way – stick together, and watch each other's backs. There's a storm coming.'

TWELFTH

**In which PT Cruiser opens up
about his nemesis, and we encounter
the astonishing Chamber of Combustion**

Up at MOTH, PT Cruiser reclined in his unicorn-leather chair, deep in contemplation. Since Project Daughter had told him about the white figure's reappearance, he'd had a whole weekend of mental turmoil.

What was it his yoga guru used to say? 'The mind is a flower. Water it with calming thoughts.' No wonder he'd had him thrown out by his ponytail.

And to think the past week had gone so well. He'd completed development on his latest Xenon DLC: 'Wash Your Bum & Armpits!' Players would soon stop performing basic cleaning functions in the real world and start doing them in Xenon instead. Personal hygiene would disappear from Bunsfold within a week, making it easier than ever to detect those few clean souls who'd resisted his bidding. Or, more usually, badding.

But as he'd feared – or was it *hoped*? – just as his plans were all coming together, his inscrutable nemesis had appeared once again. Curse the ashen-suited speed merchant! Damn his perfect racing lines, his imperviousness to fear, his resistance to being understood!

Calm, PT, he told himself. This was all for the best.

Every game needs a quest.

Cruiser finally stood up and signalled to his ugly and unreliable henchman, Maurice Marina.

'There is a boy. In my daughter's class. I want him under Cruiser Corps Level 28 surveillance from tomorrow.'

'Level 28, boss? You mean . . . switch the lethal and indescribably evil Deathbot from "Sleeper Mode" to "Active Mission Mode"? And get it to follow this kid's *every single little move*?'

'What's the use of a code name,' said PT quietly, 'IF YOU JUST SAY IT ALL ANYWAY?'

'Yes, boss. Sorry, boss. Level 28. The Deathbot will be pleased, eh? Think it's been getting a bit bored skulking around the town in disguise. Er . . . what's the kid's name?'

'Sam Wheeler.'

'Wheeler. Okey dokey. Just him, then? Not the spiky Harrison one? Wiv da stuffed animals?'

'No threat. Too dim. Did you see his maths result?'

Maurice nodded his head. Then shook it. 'But he don't play the game, boss. Like the American boy. Ain't that dangerous?'

'Have faith, Maurice. The occupant of Cell Fifteen is close to breaking point. The short one is in hand. I just need you to watch the Wheeler boy. And we must on no account let him suspect: I need him out there.'

'Out there,' nodded Maurice. And then, 'Why?'

'It seems he may have some connection to The . . . The . . . '

'The The.'

'The Stig, Maurice! My nemesis! He and this new boy are connected in some way. My own research confirms this theory. Small blips in the space–time continuum would indicate that The Stig is shadowing him . . .'

He looked at Maurice and realised he may as well be talking to himself. 'Never mind. All we know is, we need him as bait.'

'Bait. Yes.'

'If you really can't stop repeating the last word I say, maybe remain silent.'

Maurice made the sign of zipping his lip. And then: 'Silent.'

'Right, that's it!'

PT strode off down the endless corridor that bisected Cruiser Hall.

To his left were row upon row of giant data banks, containing information on every single person who had ever played Xenon.

Cruiser once again congratulated himself on the simple elegance of his instantly addictive computer game.

Xenon roamed across your brain like a spider, sucking out everything it found there.

Likes. Dislikes. Loves. Hates. Favourite colour. Favourite root vegetable.

And PT Cruiser's personal favourite: your deepest, darkest fears.

Within moments of playing, Xenon knew everything. There wasn't a locked room in your head it couldn't enter. But that was just the start. Because once it knew your wants and needs it instantly shaped itself to meet them, thereby making itself even more addictive. And once it knew your fears . . . well, anything was possible.

Yes, through Xenon he could learn everything he needed to know about anyone. And knowledge could quickly be turned into money . . . and power.

He strode on.

To the left, members of Cruiser's dog-catcher patrol prepared their latest weapons.

A minor irritation had arisen whereby Buster Mustang's troublesome pooch had taken it upon itself to interfere with the Grand Plan.

It barked at new Xenon users, breaking the software's spider-grip on their minds. It attacked Cruiser's droids like an *animal* as they carried out their daily duties. It left little 'presents' on the lenses of the Overstuffed Black Bin surveillance cameras. It even launched foolish raids on the mansion to find and liberate its master. Well, this bothersome Best Friend had messed with PT for the last time. A curse upon the hound and his ludicrous one-dog mission to scupper Project Xenon.

PT surveyed his latest helicopter gunship with its delicious meat-flavoured dog net and thought, not for the first time, of a line he looked forward to using any day now.

'Oh, you may have *the last bark*,' he'd sneer at the most

irritating Best Friend in town, 'but the *last laugh* goes to . . . PT!'

No, he had to admit it still didn't quite work. But he had enough teams of writers working on it to be confident that, when the time came, he would be equal to the task. When all was said and done, he'd only be talking to a dog.

Meanwhile, on a platform above, his chief technical officer was completing wind-tunnel testing of the latest Cruiser Narnium go-kart, destined to propel Cabriola to victory in the upcoming Bunsfold TT race. Suddenly his choice of name for the Daughter – taught to race by the greatest racing drivers he could buy – seemed an almost inspired decoy. Whoever would expect a Cabriola Cruiser to be any use at anything at all?

Finally he arrived at an electronic security door that, on strictest instructions, only PT himself – and the ever-present Maurice – were permitted to approach.

As the gate slid silently open, they entered a large room furnished with just a leather armchair, a box of Wagon Wheels and eight life-size portraits of . . .

The Stig.

Cruiser gazed at his nemesis for some time. Then, without warning, exclaimed, 'Come, come, Mr The Stig! You disappoint me! We are really not so different, you and I.'

And then . . .

'Expect you to talk? No, Mr The Stig. I expect you to drive!'

Too formal. He tried a different approach.

'So, The. Call me PT. Let's get around the football table,

kick things around a bit, run our differences up the pole and . . .'

Too try-hard. This wasn't going well.

Maurice coughed. 'Um, boss?'

'What *is* it, Maurice?'

''Scuse me, but what is it wiv this geezer? I mean, what's so special about some nutbag in white?'

PT stared into the distance.

'Perfect, crystalline focus. The Stig exists only to race. For him, everything else is just . . . waiting.'

His eyes glazed over. He paused, reminiscing. Then, 'We were almost friends once. Rivals, certainly. But with a healthy respect for each other's genius. At least I thought that's what it was. The silence, the indifference to opinion, the same monochrome outfit every day: mine black, his white.'

'Sounds like respect to me, boss.'

'It does, doesn't it? Then why must he continue to VEX me so?'

Maurice looked frustrated. 'Boss. Listen. Why don't I take a few of the guys, load 'em up wiv machine guns, stand in front of our friend Mr The Stig here and just let him 'ave it? Eh? Job done. *Hasta la vista,* Stiggo.'

Cruiser looked put out. 'No, Maurice! Whatever you do, never machine-gun him at close range with automatic weapons. It only makes him cross. No . . . I have other plans for our mysterious friend.'

He smiled a dangerous smile, then reached down and pulled a concealed lever by his chair.

Instantly the wall panel to his right slid upwards, revealing a giant cylindrical mechanism, breathtaking in its scope and majesty.

Cruiser surveyed his deadly motorised masterpiece with awe. For here towered the Engine from the End of the World: the nightmarish Chamber of Combustion.

Finally. The means to rid himself of He Who Shall Never Remove His Helmet.

Some said it was the only way to destroy him. Termination by Engine! What could be more appropriate?

He sensed his prey was near. All that remained was to lure him into a trap so fiendishly attractive that not even he would be able to resist.

From deep within, and despite himself, Cruiser once again felt the distant stirrings of respect for his mute adversary. A nemesis seemingly immune to both pain and pleasure. An opponent wholly unshakeable in purpose. An enemy that – no matter how overwhelming the temptation – would never, ever pick his nose.

But enough!

He gazed once more at his helmeted foe, thrust his arms aloft and, trembling with fury, found his authentic voice.

'Inlet! Spark! Combustion! Behold . . . we shall exhaust him!'

THIRTEENTH

*In which we finally discover Harrison's first name,
and learn about the Wotsits Challenge*

The indescribably complex and evil machine known as the Deathbot checked its circuits. Active Mission Mode at last. *That* felt better. And, already, a data blip.

LEVEL 28 SURVEILLANCE TARGET NEARBY . . .
ACT . . . NATURAL . . .

Blissfully unaware that he was being stalked by the most dangerous machine ever devised, Sam Wheeler walked to school, determined that things would get better. At least they couldn't get much worse.

Or so he thought.

Once again, things hadn't started well. Everywhere he looked he saw signs of the Cruiser Corporation's sinister presence.

Black helicopters buzzing in and out of MOTH. A traffic jam stretching all the way down Bombshell Drive as two workmen with STOP/GO signs stared at their hand-held computers instead of waving the traffic through.

Someone, thought Sam, wanted things like this. But what he couldn't figure out was . . . why?

He trudged past long lines of school-run parents with

their Xenon-addicted children. Precisely none of them were enjoying the traditional pastime known as 'looking out of the window'.

Quicker on a bike, he thought as he gazed at the stuck cars, and just for an instant wished he was riding instead of walking. But he wasn't ready to get back in the saddle yet. He wasn't sure he ever would be. Gramps was badly injured, and it had all been his fault.

He heard a noise behind him, and turned to see the now familiar sight of a small kid huffing and puffing on an old-style bicycle far too large for him. Harrison! His determined riding style reminded Sam of a famous cyclist from the past, though he couldn't remember who.

That was it. Mary Poppins.

As the bike didn't look set to catch up any time soon, Sam decided to wait. 'Morning, Harrison,' he called out. 'Stuffed any marsupials into rubbish bins lately?'

Harrison looked flustered. 'Er . . . no,' he said, looking around nervously. 'I mean, come on, Wheeler, why would anyone want to do a crazy thing like . . . ?'

'Call me Wheels,' said Sam. 'And, talking of crazy things, I don't know your first name.'

The kid just stood there, leaning against his outsized bike and panting.

'So?' said Sam eventually.

'So what?'

'What's your first name?'

The small kid caught his breath. Finally, he turned to Sam and said, 'Ford. My first name is Ford.'

'Ford Harrison?' guffawed Sam. 'Was your parents' first date to see *Wars Star*? Or let me guess – your mum's a big fan of *Jones Indiana*?'

'No,' said the small kid. 'Mondeos, actually.'

'Really?'

'I was born in one. Deep Impact Blue, titanium trim. On the way to hospital. Six weeks early. They couldn't very well call me Mondeo, so Ford it is.'

'And you realise your name sounds like a film star in reverse, right?' said Sam.

'He starred in *Sraw Rats*,' said a voice behind them.

'Minnie!' said Sam. 'Where did you spring from?'

'On my way to school, like you,' she replied. 'As for Ford here, I suspect he's not the MOT failure he likes to make out. He could be a Model T pupil. He just needs to Focus.'

My kind of girl, thought Sam for the umpteenth time, and joined in.

'Are you saying,' he replied, 'he's Cortina trap and we need to Escort him out of it?'

He and Minnie attempted a high-five, but started giggling instead.

'If Fiesta listen to much more of this, I'll explode,' said Minnie.

'Well, I think Ford is a fantastic first name,' said Sam. 'All joking aside.'

'Really?' said Harrison suspiciously.

'Absolutely,' replied Sam. 'One of the best in the Galaxy.'

'Stop it now, seriously,' said Minnie. 'He's S-Maxed out.'

'You're right,' said Sam. 'Let's talk about something else. Going anywhere nice on your holidays?'

'Granada?' said Minnie. 'In the High Sierra?' And the two of them collapsed in giggles all over again.

Seeing Harrison looking grumpy, Sam made a determined effort to hold things together.

'Ford. I'm sorry. I couldn't help it . . . Let's change the subject. So, where *are* you going on hols?'

Ford paused. Then, 'Capri,' he admitted.

At which point Sam and Minnie howled with laughter.

'You can't be serious,' said Sam, wiping tears from his eyes.

'I'm not, you idiot,' said Ford. 'Ka we stop now . . . ?'

But he was cut off by a bicycle overtaking them at a dangerous lick, and nearly taking Sam's lunchbox with it.

'Charade!' spat Ford and Minnie.

'What . . . ?' asked Sam as the bike sped out of sight.

'Dennis Charade,' said Ford. 'Proper pain in the bum. He's on an Apprentice Bullyship with Cabriola's gang, but working hard on Full Member status. And in the meantime he's polishing his porkies.'

Sam gave a look that said, 'Huh?'

'He's the class fibber,' explained Minnie. 'You know how there's always one kid at school that reckons he's had a trial for Arsenal? Or says Simon Cowell is his second cousin? Or that his dad used to fly the space shuttle before packing it all in to be a minicab driver? Well, at Bunsfold High, that's Dennis Charade.'

They were at the gates by now, where the skinny, weasel-like kid was waiting for them. Rodent eyes darted left and right as he spoke.

'Better man up, new boy,' he sneered nasally. 'Today's the Wotsits Challenge, and the Cruiser Crew are waiting for you.'

'Excellent,' said Sam flatly. 'And what's the Wotsits Challenge exactly? I can see you're dying to tell me.'

'Don't worry – you'll find out,' said Charade breathlessly, before lifting his rear wheel in a well-rehearsed but clumsy attempt at a double tail whip.

'Wonderful,' shot back Sam, his heart sinking fast. 'And terrific bike control, by the way.'

'It should be. Watch and learn, new kid. I took Gold in the last National Championships.'

Which Sam knew from personal experience was a load of cobblers.

'Even though my leg was in plaster,' added Dennis, as if he'd just thought it up.

With that, he rode off towards a crowd of kids on the far side of the playground. Sam turned to his new mates.

'So, which one of you is going to tell me?'

Ford made a show of looking innocent. Minnie made a rubbish attempt at whistling a jaunty tune.

Sam persevered. 'The Wotsits Challenge?'

'You're racing Cabriola around the school on bikes,' Ford admitted. 'Winner gets a packet of Wotsits or comparable cheese snack of his or her choice.'

As Sam approached the playing field, he heard cheering, closely followed by laughter. And there, in the middle of the throng, awaited his own personal nemesis.

'Ah, new kid. We've been expecting you,' said another familiar voice. 'Come on down.'

FOURTEENTH

**In which Sam appears to turn chicken,
and everything takes a turn for the worse**

Cabriola Cruiser was sitting astride the slickest bike Sam had ever seen – the 'wow' BMX from the first day. Taking a closer look this time, Sam instantly clocked suspension forks he'd only read about on the real geek forums, and several other parts he'd never even imagined possible.

'Welcome to the track. Bit of a new-kid ritual,' said Cabriola, smiling and staring hard at Sam while pulling a black leather riding glove on each hand.

Spooner bounced up and down like a ferret on a pogo stick and grinned expectantly, his hand on the saddle of a bike far too small for him.

'We call it the Wotsits Challenge,' said Cabriola. 'You race me around the school, winner gets a pack of cheese-flavoured snacks. And other equally cheesy things like prestige and bragging rights and so on. Probably. Nobody's ever beaten me, but I imagine that's what would happen. Ready?'

Despite himself, Sam was still inspecting Cabriola's BMX. What was that seat post made of? Not carbon. Not titanium. No material he recognised. He couldn't help reaching out to touch it, but as he did so it seemed to grow spikes like a cranky cactus. When he drew his hand away, they disappeared. What *was* this stuff?

'Nothing you've ever heard of, new kid,' sneered Spooner. 'We've code-named it . . . Narnium!'

Sam burst out laughing. 'Narnium! What kind of stupid name is that? What's the bell made of? Lord of the Ringsium?'

He leaned over to check out the rear tyre, but Cabriola lifted a hand to his chest. 'Don't bother checking out the back. You'll be seeing plenty of it in a minute.'

Sam turned away, not in the mood for yet another scrape. 'I won't, actually,' he said, and began to walk away.

'Hummer!' snapped Cabriola.

The giant walking hoody stepped straight into Sam's path.

Sam gazed up at him. 'Why, Hummer,' he said, 'I see they've taught you to stand on your hind legs.'

Cabriola stared at Sam. 'You don't get away that easily, Hippy Hair. I'm challenging you to a race. Local rules, old sport. You have to accept. Unless, of course, you're –'

'Not today,' said Sam. 'I don't have a ride.'

'It's height rear,' piped up Spooner, lifting the MTB towards Sam.

'Right here,' said Cabriola with an icy smile.

'Thanks, but not today,' said Sam, more insistently.

'Bake the tike,' said Spooner menacingly. Ford Harrison was eyeing Sam closely with a puzzled look on his face as if something wasn't adding up. Sam spoke firmly.

'Some other time.'

'Some other time?' mocked Charade. 'What does that mean?'

Minnie was looking at Sam as if expecting another nifty put-down. But instead he just said, quietly but firmly, 'It means I can't ride a bike.'

Silence. And then the laughter erupted.

Minnie Cooper and Ford Harrison quickly looked away.

Sam spluttered and went very red. 'I don't mean I can't *ride a bike*. I mean I just can't ride one *now* . . .'

But nobody heard.

Cabriola held up her hand for silence. Her face was so close their noses almost touched.

She stood there for a good ten seconds, calculating. That may not sound like much, but it's a whole lot of silence for a full school playground.

Finally she sneered. 'Ha! I've seen more spine on a worm farm.'

Then she leaned forward to whisper to Sam, so no one else could hear. 'What's the point of having a tame racing driver for a guardian angel, if he doesn't turn up when you need him?'

Sam felt his face burning, and turned away quickly so his tormentor wouldn't see.

'You see, Mr *Wheels*?' said Cabriola. 'Mess with me and you get kerbed.'

She turned to Minnie. 'Guess he's not the guy you thought he was,' she said evenly. 'But, then again, he's exactly the guy I thought he was.'

Then she, Spooner and Hummer headed in to school. Nobody moved until Cabriola called over her shoulder, 'Time for school, children. Run along.'

The crowd dispersed. Nobody looked at Sam.

Except the spiky-haired Ford Harrison, who stood there shaking his head from side to side like an iguana watching tennis.

FIFTEENTH

In which Sam gets a tricycle, Ford gets cross and The Stig gets named

Word travelled fast, and for the rest of the morning it seemed like every kid in Bunsfold was queuing up to take a cheap shot at Sam.

Not that he cared. Well, maybe a bit.

But there were people at Bunsfold High he *did* care about. And was it just him, or were they suddenly being a bit distant?

Ford Harrison nodded as Sam walked past him into their English lesson, but that was it.

Sam sat down and leaned over to Minnie's desk. 'So . . . where does Spiderman shop?' he asked breezily. But today even she wasn't playing. She looked up, but said nothing.

They were doing *Animal Farm,* near the end, the bit where the pigs write *Four legs good, two legs better* on the barn, and just for a moment Sam lost himself in the story. Mean creatures controlling everyone and keeping the best for themselves – then persuading the others it was for their own good. It all sounded pretty familiar to this recent resident of Bunsfold. He looked over at Cabriola, only to jump with a start when he caught his blonde nemesis staring straight back at him. She was nodding.

'That's right,' she seemed to say. 'Welcome to *my* farm.'

And then his spirits really sank: lunchtime. He had to pick up his PE kit from the locker – where, predictably, another side-splitting prank awaited.

Parked in front of it was a toddler tricycle, with pink ribbons and a My Little Pony decal on the crossbar. There was a note stuck to the saddle: *IF LOST, PLEASE RETURN TO THIS LOSER – SAM 'THREE' WHEELER.*

He looked up and saw Minnie Cooper closing her own locker, a few metres away.

'Ride 'em, cowboy,' she said, and smiled sympathetically. She walked off towards the dining hall, then stopped for a moment and turned back. 'Oh, and one other thing,' she said. 'On the web.'

And she was gone.

Yup, thought Sam, that is indeed where Spiderman shops.

And, though outwardly calm, in his mind he was triumphantly knee-sliding the entire length of the corridor. Things were getting the tiniest bit better.

Then he checked his timetable.

Strike that. Double maths.

The fragrant Mr Rodius was on the warpath. As soon as he saw the three of them in class, he exploded.

'Harrison! Cooper! New boy! Did I not instruct you to visit the headmaster?'

'We did, sir,' said Minnie.

'And yet here you are, still in school. Did he not suspend you?'

'No, sir. He just gave us some advice and sent us on our way,' said Minnie, flatly.

'Advice? I've never heard anything so lily-livered. What about?'

'I'm afraid we're not allowed to tell you, sir,' said Minnie. Sam grimaced. So it was true, he thought. Minnie Cooper clearly didn't scare easily. But the tone of that reply sounded ever so bold.

He was right. Rodius smiled dangerously, crossed his arms and murmured menacingly, 'I see, Miss Cooper. So what *would* you like to tell me about?'

'I'm sorry, sir,' said Minnie. 'I really don't know what you mean.'

'I mean, Miss Cooper, that if you're refusing to impart information on *that* particular subject, then pick another. And I shall test you on it. And, if you fail, you shall be graded a C-minus and returned to the headmaster so that he might reconsider that suspension.'

Minnie looked at him blankly.

'Cat got your tongue? Hmm? Now come, come, Miss Cooper. You must have a special subject of some sort. Music, perhaps? Ted Sheeran? Taylor Shift?'

Minnie looked confused. 'Well, I do like cars, engines, that sort of thing, I suppose.'

My sort of girl, thought Sam Wheeler to himself. Not for the first time.

'Engines! Splendid. So perhaps you can tell me the biggest

engine ever fitted to a production car?'

Once again, Minnie looked blank. But Rodius was just warming up.

'No? How about the biggest-selling engine of all time? Or the largest? Or the most powerful?'

Once again, Minnie just stared.

'So,' the smirking teacher finally said, 'not so finely tuned after all, Miss Cooper? C-minus.'

At which point Ford Harrison – whose spiky head had scarcely appeared from behind a textbook all term – once again jumped to his feet. But this time he was angry.

Very angry.

Enough, it seemed, was finally enough. And his voice – now strangely calm and flat – rang across the classroom.

'You haven't told us the answers yet.'

Every face in the class swung to the back of the class. It was, after all, only the second time most of them had heard their all-but-invisible classmate say anything at all.

Rodius looked ready to explode.

Sam put his head in his hands. Here we go again, he thought.

'I'll get to *YOU* in a minute,' snapped the teacher. 'Now sit back down. And the rest of you turn to –'

But Ford Harrison interrupted him again. And he hadn't sat down. 'So what exactly was the biggest engine in a production car?' He paused. 'Sir?'

Rodius stuttered, and looked as if he was about to catch fire. Ford continued.

'Mr Rodius. You appear a little confused. The biggest engine in a production car was 13,503 CC in the 1912 Pierce-Arrow Model 6-66 Raceabout. The most powerful engine was the NASA F-1 for the Saturn 5 rocket with 32 million bhp. The largest engine in the world is the MWe ARABELLE turbine generator in a French nuclear power station – and the biggest-selling engine ever is the Honda Super Cub, which passed 60 million sales in 2008.'

He paused again.

'Sir.'

An awed silence fell over the room. Minnie and Sam stared at Ford, their mouths agape. Rodius now bore the expression of a stuffed meerkat, and then did what he always did when he was flummoxed. And it smelled of cheese and Brussels sprouts.

As the bell went, most of the class scrambled for fresh air. Sam was about to do the same when he noticed Minnie still sitting there, calmly putting her books in order. The only kid cool enough to withstand a full-power Rodius guff-bubble without gagging. He opened the nearest window and said, 'You okay?'

'Never better,' she replied. 'Ford, that was impressive. Thanks.'

'You can say that again,' added Sam. 'How did you know all that stuff?'

Ford looked irritated with himself. 'It was mostly bluff, to be perfectly honest. Why don't I just *grow up*?'

'Well, you're certainly growing on me.' Minnie smiled.

Sam looked hard at Ford. 'I think you've just blown your cover, mate, haven't you?' he said quietly.

Ford looked sideways, with a suspiciously 'Oh-no-I've-just-been-rumbled' expression. Sam was confused. Why would anyone work so hard to look like the class dummy when they weren't even remotely the class dummy?

Then again, he thought to himself, nothing made any sense in this crazy place.

'Great,' he sighed. 'Just great. So in my first week I discover a billionaire girl-bully, a psycho maths teacher, Peter Perfect missing in the forest, "dark forces" loose in the town and a storm coming. Not forgetting the loony in a white racing suit who's apparently been protecting my family for years. I'm beginning to suspect Bunsfold was built on the site of an ancient Apache burial ground, and –'

But before he could finish his sentence, Sam noticed that Minnie was suddenly staring at him very hard, her large dark eyes even larger and darker than usual.

Then, quietly and carefully, she asked, 'Did you say a loony in a white racing suit?'

Sam said nothing, and Minnie added, 'What do you mean, *protecting your family for years*?'

Sam's mind was racing. Gramps had told him to keep the Spitfire story quiet, but . . . well, somehow he knew this was important. And he was beginning to suspect he could trust these two, after all.

He made a decision.

He took a deep breath. Instantly regretted it. What *was* Rodius dining on, exactly? Rushing to the window, he filled his lungs with non-polluted air and expelled it at a speed entirely appropriate to his next four words;

'He's called The Stig.'

SIXTEENTH

In which PT Cruiser opens up
about his history with The Stig

Back up at MOTH, PT Cruiser was busy boring the trousers off his most trusted employee.

'Maurice,' he began, 'have I ever told you why I'm so bothered by The . . . The . . . Oh, you know. Him.'

'Him.'

'The Stig.'

'No, boss. Never.'

Actually he'd heard the story several hundred times. But he understood when he needed to be a Good Listener.

'Well, sit yourself down. I think that time has finally come.'

PT Cruiser sighed, misty-eyed. Maurice sighed, bleary-eyed.

'It all began in the last year of college back in California. My classmates and I were just millionaires back then, of course. Barely two helicopters to rub together. Everything seemed so much *simpler,* you know?'

'Simpler, boss. I know.'

'And then, out of nowhere, I had an idea for just the funnest video game ever, where the cutest eeniest-weeniest puppies would wake up, climb out of their baskets, have a cute little stretch and then wander across a highway busy with oncoming Heavy Goods Vehicles.'

'Might that have been, boss, the very same idea that became Puppy Truck Death Race 2000, the biggest-selling video game of that same year?'

'Ha!' laughed PT, throwing his head back. 'Well yes, Maurice, now that you mention it. But first I needed to see it work in real life. So I invested in a pedigree puppy-breeding farm built right next to a busy highway.

'We agreed it'd be a great prank to let all the dogs out and bet on which breeds had least road sense. I had a cool hundred thou on the Jack Russell, but most of the action was around the Shi-Tzu and the Peke. Dumb as cats, apparently. We all wanted the glory of opening the gates and scaring 'em toward the road, so we decided to race there. Usual rules . . . last one in the lobby buys the hotel. The kennels were just outside Las Vegas, around three hundred miles and a full tank of gas away. It was . . . perfect.'

'We met up at Long Beach in some pretty mundane imported kit: Porsches, Maseratis, a few tweaked Ferraris. I was in my shopping runaround, a tastefully modified Lamborghini Countach Estate, and felt quietly confident. Then, just around the start time, this extra car appeared. Not much to look at. A '69 Dodge Charger with around 425 horses at the back wheel that just had to handle like a bronco with toothache.'

He paused for a moment. 'But then there was . . . *the driver.*'

He paused again, his expression flitting between contempt, respect, fear, trapped wind, loathing, admiration then back to contempt and round again.

'He was this dude in a white suit and helmet. Quiet guy, unassuming, so we let him ride alongside all the way to the start of Highway 15. Then as the towns gave way to open road we strung out, and he disappeared.

'I was well in the lead at the Nevada state line, but just in case I switched a few signs behind me and spilled some oil on a few of the more dangerous bends. Basic insurance, you know? Nothing elaborate.'

'Basic, boss,' agreed the henchman.

'Anyway, long story short, most of my pals crashed and burned as expected, but the kid in the Dodge was somehow actually *catching me up* as Vegas came in sight. So I deployed the Lambo's main race mod, the massive arm that comes out the back and lifts the other driver out of his . . . You know the one, right?'

'Right, boss. Standard.'

'Well, he somehow avoided it without crashing his ridiculous antique machine, came up the inside and, well, sort of . . .'

'Won a heroic victory against overwhelming odds, boss?' said Maurice.

'. . . reached the finish line outside the farm before I did. He'd won the right to release the infant hounds! But, instead, you know what he did?'

'No idea. None whatsoever.'

'He went right up to the front door and – get this – shoved a giant padlock across it, so none of us could . . . *Aaaargh!* It still vexes me to this day. Then back in his car, straight round and right back out of town.

'But not before banging on the door to get the goody-two-shoes kennel manager out to see what was going on. So bang went our plan. And I never did get to see if my hunch about Jack Russells was right.

'And, ever since, the guy has had it in for me. Can't explain it: just one of those things. Turns up at the tiniest suggestion of World Domination, thwarts my plans, disappears. But, as I say, I think he respects me. He respects me, right, Maurice? As a worthy opponent? Because that's what I am. Right?'

'Right, boss. Anyone would think that.'

'I don't want to THINK! I need to KNOW! And that's what really gets to me, Maurice. I can find out anything about anyone. You play Xenon – I learn about you, I own you. You play more – I have more control. Everybody's happy. But how can you deal with someone unknowable? Sure, *some say* he's indifferent to Marmite – and that his smiles are vertical – but they don't KNOW!'

PT collapsed, sobbing.

Knowledge was all. And when it came to The Stig, knowledge was almost entirely AWOL.

Except for one ever-present fact. The Stig lived to race. Couldn't resist. The higher the stakes, the more certain it was that he'd turn up for a challenge. And these stakes were the highest *ever.* The upcoming Bunsfold TT might look like a go-kart race around a sleepy Surrey one-horse town, but in fact it was the soft launch of a viral mind-control machine that would change humanity forever.

PT lifted his head from the desk. He clenched a fist. He tried a *Mwa-ha-haaa.*

Maurice had begun to snore quietly.

He'd have to work on that.

SEVENTEENTH

**In which Sam and Minnie meet Ford's mum,
and make for a rather special shed**

Wednesday started slowly, until the news broke.

The headmaster had disappeared.

There were plenty of rumours. One kid said he'd been spotted at a local motel, stuck in a darkened room playing an endless game of Xenon. But the only certain thing was, as a nervous-looking Mr Hornet had announced at assembly, that Mr Leyland had been 'called away' urgently. Coming so soon after the Mustang disappearance last year, the adults were getting really jumpy.

So was Sam. Even more when Ford Harrison didn't turn up for school.

He wasn't sure why this should bother him, but it did. Sure, Ford was a bit weird. And rode his ridiculous sit-up-and-beg bicycle so slowly Sam reckoned he'd seen faster-moving roadkill. Not to mention his *absurdly* childish crush on Minnie Cooper – something Sam would never, ever surrender to. No way.

But maybe the little spiky-haired kid was growing on him. Who knew? Sam was certainly beginning to feel a bit protective of Ford. Without him, Bunsfold High seemed to contain only psychopathic bullies or zombies on games consoles.

Apart from the wonderful Minnie Cooper, of course. Who, it turned out, was thinking exactly the same thing.

'Hope Ford's all right,' she said as the last lesson of a long day spent avoiding the Crew finally drew to a close. 'Quite missed him today.'

'You read my mind,' said Sam.

'I wish I could,' replied the Cooper, in a way that made him feel just a little bit like there was a tap dance going on in his tummy.

He made a decision.

'Let's go and find out how he is. Where's he live?'

'I know the street,' said Minnie. 'Not the number, though.'

'Leave that to me,' said Sam. 'I'll knock on a few doors.'

So it was that fifteen minutes later – or about twenty by bicycle, if your name's Ford Harrison – the two of them marched up the pathway of an ordinary house on the edge of the forest with a dark blue Ford Mondeo Estate parked on the driveway.

A glamorous middle-aged woman in a smart dress opened the door.

'Hello, Mrs Harrison,' said Minnie. 'Is Ford in?'

'Why, is something wrong?'

'We're friends of his. From school,' said Sam.

'Friends? Are you sure?'

'Quite sure,' said Minnie firmly. 'Hello, by the way. I'm Minnie Cooper.'

The woman immediately brightened.

'*The* Minnie Cooper? I'm so sorry! Come in, dear! You're much taller than you look in Ford's scrapbook. And who's this handsome long-haired gentleman? Haven't seen *you* tagged in any of his photostreams. Or maybe you're more of a Snapchat kinda guy, eh?'

And she gave what looked like an actual wink. Could have been a tic, thought Sam kindly, but it looked very wink-like from where he was standing.

'Sam Wheeler,' said Sam. 'I'm new.'

'Well, come on through, my loves. Sorry to be a bit slow on the uptake, but Ford doesn't have visitors very often. Or ever, actually. He used to spend a lot of time with that handsome young American chap, getting up to all sorts, but since he went away Ford seems to spend every evening in his shed working on his inventions. Terribly clever. Gets it from his Uncle Bob, I think.'

'Lovely!' said Minnie brightly, following her through to the living room. 'You have a brother? Wish I did!'

'Yes, dear. Awfully brainy, just like Ford, bless him. Not that he gets any credit for it at that appalling school.'

Just then, a door slammed and a familiar voice called from the kitchen.

'Mum! Hungry! Dinner, please! Need to get back to the shed! Still working on my physics proje . . .'

Then Ford Harrison walked in, saw Sam and Minnie on the sofa and reeled backwards in shock.

'Ford my darling, your friends just popped in to check up on you. Isn't that sweet? Sit down, dear. I'll get dinner in a minute. So, where was I? Oh yes. Terribly clever but always small for his age . . .'

Ford stirred himself. 'Mum, please don't do that thing.'

'What thing, dear?'

'That thing when you talk about me as if I'm not in the room, when I am.'

'I'm not, dear.'

'And then say something incredibly embarrassing.'

'Wouldn't dream of it, my love. Now, where was I? That's right. Lovely boy, but always terribly *little*. Apart from his digestive tract, funnily enough, which must be huge because his number twos have always been simply *enormous* . . .'

'Mum!' yelled Ford.

'His uncle used to say it looked as if a passing bison had wandered into the bathroom.'

'MUM!'

'Sorry,' said Mrs Harrison. 'Forget I said that.'

With a growing dread, Sam realised he never would.

Ford had had enough.

'Okay, thanks, Mum. Let's skip tea – not hungry, thanks. I'll take Sam and Minnie upstairs to my bedroom.'

'As you please,' said his mum, 'but, just so you know, I'm hosting my book club this evening. We're reading this terribly exciting yarn called . . .'

'Okay, okay. Then I'll take them to . . .' and he paused for a moment, as if in an argument with himself. Then, decisively: 'I'll take them to the shed.'

'Well! Lucky you two!' said his mum. 'None of us are ever allowed to see it. All right, off you pop. Lovely to meet.'

'Thanks, Mrs H,' said Minnie as they jumped up to leave. And then, in a whisper, 'Love the earrings.'

As soon as they were out of sight, Ford stopped and turned to his companions.

'Sorry about that. So, what's this about?'

'The headmaster's disappeared,' said Sam. 'No one's got a clue what's happened to him.'

Ford stood still and stared into the distance. But he didn't look surprised.

'That confirms it,' he said quietly, and to no one in particular.

'Confirms what?' said Minnie.

'Xenon,' said Ford. 'He was on to it.' Then, after a pause, he looked hard at Sam and Minnie. 'You still haven't played it, have you? Either of you?'

They each shook their heads, though Minnie wrinkled up her nose and looked a bit put out.

'Aren't we all being a bit paranoid about Xenon? I mean, it's only a computer game.'

Ford didn't answer, but simply handed them a scarf each.

'What's this?' said Sam.

'Blindfold.'

'Uh . . . why?' said Minnie.

'Secret den. Wouldn't be much of a secret if I showed you where it was, would it?'

'Ford. Are you serious? It's only a shed, for heaven's sake,' said Sam.

Ford turned to him.

'Oh, it's not a shed, Wheels. You'll see.'

Nearby, closer than they realised, the watching Deathbot's Excitement Module whirred inaudibly.

WOOHOO . . . NEW . . . INTELLIGENCE . . . IMMINENT

EIGHTEENTH

In which we enter the Den

Minnie took her scarf and tied it round her eyes. Sam reluctantly did the same. He couldn't see a thing, but listened carefully instead for clues to where he was going. He'd seen it done in a film.

First he heard a giant waterfall, quite close. Then a marching band. A large pane of glass shattering. Two wildebeest mating. A male-voice choir singing 'I Dreamed a Dream', in Welsh. Each lasted for a short blast then disappeared. What sort of place was this?

Then Ford spoke. 'Sorry. New phone. Why can't I find a ring tone that just goes *briiiiing*? Anyway, we're here. Don't just stand there. Take them off.'

As Sam removed his scarf, he gulped.

They were in a clearing. Towering over them was a huge, overgrown mound in the shape of a giant Swiss roll. Gorse bushes, leaves, scrub and dirt covered it, but in the odd patch here and there Sam clocked sun glinting off metal.

'Come on,' said Ford, striding purposefully towards the far end. 'No time to gawp.' He stopped in front of a pile of junk. Three rusty prams, a rickety stove, a bent truck axle. And, right in the middle, a Reliant Robin, which looked as if it had uncharacteristically toppled over and crashed right into the side of the mound.

Ford whipped an old TV remote from his pocket and pointed it straight at the tailgate of the Reliant.

'Welcome,' he said solemnly, '. . . to BCHQ.'

And absolutely nothing happened.

Ford pointed the control again, pressing it several times with increasing force.

Then, just as he started banging the remote on his knee, the Reliant's glass tailgate began to crank itself open.

As the dusty hatch lifted, Sam could see that the only thing inside was a bright blue kids' slide, heading out through where the front windscreen should have been and straight into the giant mound.

'You first,' Sam said to Ford.

'Sorry, got to pull the tailgate shut behind me. Go on, just slide down.'

Sam hesitated. 'Um, no thanks, Ford, I'll just . . . Oi!'

'You wuss,' said Minnie with a shove.

Sam landed with a *WHUMP* on an old leather car seat.

Then, with another *WHUMP*, Minnie appeared beside him.

Sam took off his specs to wipe away the dust they'd picked up in the tunnel.

And when he put them back on he was treated to the most amazing sight he'd seen since *The Big Book of Amazing Sights*

Gramps had given him last Christmas.

'Wow,' he said.

'OMG,' said Minnie Cooper under her breath.

They were inside a huge aircraft hangar. Scattered around were parts of engines, bikes, TVs, car magazines and every decent computer game yet invented. The remnants of a Formula Three racing-car cockpit wired up to a screen showing Gran Turismo 8. One of those grabby robot hands where instead of winning soft toy Garfields you won cold cans of ginger beer. A Penny Falls machine that actually paid out. Air hockey. There was even a vending machine for crisps, snacks and sweets with a notice taped over the coin slot saying FREE. Some remnants of a military past remained: propped up against a wall was the whole wing of an RAF fighter. In the far corner Sam recognised the bicycle trailer from the other day and, propped up inside it, a random selection of stuffed furry marsupials.

Just as Sam jumped to his feet to check everything out, Ford hurtled down with another *WHUMP* and landed right where he'd been sitting.

'Right, tailgate's shut. Don't just stand there, take a seat.'

Sam was spoiled for choice. In one corner sat what looked like a World War II bombshell, but hollowed out on one side and converted into a comfortable sofa. But he chose the other, a funny-looking padded chair that –

'NOT THAT ONE!' boomed Ford.

Sam leaped up again.

'Sorry,' said Ford. 'Ejector seat. From a Lightning jet fighter. I'm pretty sure it's properly disconnected now, but we don't want a repeat of last month's little drama.' And he glanced upwards towards a hole in the roof.

'Ford Harrison,' announced Minnie, looking around the Den and then smiling down at him with an expression of wonder. 'You *legend.*'

Ford blushed instantly, and turned away.

'Me and Buster, really.'

He hadn't said his friend's name aloud to anyone for months. It felt good, but emotional. Almost as emotional as having the real, actual Minnie Cooper right here in the flesh. Just as he'd come to the conclusion that she might indeed be his Perfect Girl. Well, in every respect bar one.

That reminded him. He hurriedly covered the blueprints for the Leg Extender, kicked the prototype Levitating Shoe further under his desk and hid the experimental jar of Project High Hair behind a pile of car magazines. Now he could concentrate.

'But . . . how . . . when . . . what?' asked Sam.

'Old aircraft hangar,' said Ford. 'Disused since the war. Bit of a mess when we found it: I think the pilots used it as a recreation room back then. But we tidied it up, camouflaged the opening and hey presto.'

'Well, I *love* what you've done with the place,' said Minnie. 'Now, where do I sit?'

'Over there,' said Ford. 'On that bombshell.'

But before she could sit down Minnie spotted something in the far corner of the Den.

'Blimey!' she exclaimed. 'What is *that*?'

There, perched on a workbench, was a bizarre contraption that looked like a cross between a scaled-down Formula One car and a pram. On the back was something that looked suspiciously like a giant vacuum cleaner.

'The Rocket,' said Ford. 'Purpose-designed for the upcoming Bunsfold TT. My personal mission to finally beat Cabriola Cruiser at her own game.'

'Beautiful,' said Sam. 'How does she go?'

'Properly quick in a straight line and just about un-drivable everywhere else, I'm afraid.' He paused for a moment. 'But then it does seem to be getting better.'

He paused again, and frowned. 'Which is very strange.'

'Why?' asked Minnie.

'Because I haven't touched it. But I could swear it's being . . . tweaked.'

'How?'

'I wish I knew. But every time I come back, the handling's got better.'

'Must be magic,' said Minnie.

'Or elves,' said Sam, deadpan. 'You know, the little friendly folk that helped the shoemaker in the fairy tale.'

'Of course. Why on earth didn't we think of that?' said Minnie. 'Little friendly elves. Taken the whole shoe thing as far as they can, now moving on to engine tweaks and handling upgrades. Obvious, when you think about it.'

Ford stuck to his guns.

'Well, someone's been working on it. And another thing. Whoever it is leaves a series of strange smells. Just last night I came back and there it was. The unmistakable whiff of . . . orphan badger cub.'

Minnie's ears pricked up.

'Always the same smell?'

'Now you mention it, no,' said Ford. 'Sometimes it's more like . . . an unstuck plaster? Why so interested?'

Minnie looked at him, then at the Rocket, then spoke.

'Right,' she said. 'Time we got organised. Let's find out everything we can about the Man of Mystery in the white racing suit. The . . . Sprig, was it?'

'Stig,' said Sam. 'He's called The Stig.'

'That's it,' said Minnie. 'The Stig. I'm beginning to suspect he could be the answer to a lot of things around here.'

NINETEENTH

**In which we start to find out more
and end up knowing less.
That's The Stig for you**

The three friends loaded up with ginger beer and snacks, and each took turns at the keyboard. But, two hours later, it seemed The Stig existed without trace. A ghost. A phantom. A dead end.

The trio had roamed the vast, rolling plains of the internet and crossed oceans of YouTube seeking even the teensiest sign, and drawn nothing but a dark-visored blank.

But if Sam's story was true, then the authorities had known all about the White Helmet for more than seventy years.

The authorities! Of course!

Ford's Uncle Bob worked for the government. Probably the smartest spy in the top secret Department of Smart Spies, Uncle Bob was a brilliant boffin who had devoted his entire career to . . . well, Ford had absolutely no idea. That was sort of the point.

But whatever Bob's special area of expertise might be, he had to have access to government files. Ford just needed to pose as him and find a way in.

Getting into the system wouldn't be easy. He soon found his uncle was Security Clearance Level 10, and all his documents were protected by weapons-grade firewalls. But Ford had the advantage of spending every Christmas with his subject.

He typed the name of Uncle Bob's West Highland terrier into the password box.

O-D-D-J-O-B.

Ha! Bang. They were in. 'And . . . Bob's my uncle!' he proclaimed triumphantly.

'Ford, you're a *genius,*' said Minnie.

'I don't get it, Harrison,' said Sam, looking puzzled. 'At school you're as dense as a cricket ball, and about as talkative. And you score the first-ever zero in a science exam. Then outside you build this amazing den and a go-kart and hack in to secret government files. What gives?'

Ford paused for a moment. 'I'm in a war zone,' he said, suddenly looking deadly serious. 'When in hostile territory, always convince the enemy you're not a threat. Because if they underestimate you, they'll probably ignore you.'

'I get it,' said Minnie. 'You're the Resistance, hiding in plain sight.'

'Well, now *we* are,' said Ford. 'The three of us.' And he hit OPEN FILES. 'Let's see what's in here.'

They leaned in.

There were all manner of fascinating secret government papers to explore in there. But Ford resisted the temptation to dip into the 'ELVIS IS TOTALLY STILL ALIVE' and 'THE

WORLD IS BEING SECRETLY RUN BY SCALY ALIEN LIZARD CREATURES' files. He had far more important things to investigate.

Two hours of digging later, there was still no trace. There remained one lone document with a long, peculiar title: GITS EHT TUOBA WONK EW LLA.

'Someone's been cleaning the keyboard,' said Sam. 'My turn.'

Ford reached for a last gulp of his drink. And as he raised it to his lips he had one of those moments you only get a few times in a life.

Mirrored back in the glass tumbler, the title made perfect sense.

ALL WE KNOW ABOUT THE STIG.

Sam and Minnie leaned further in, breathless with anticipation. Ford Harrison took a deep breath to steady himself.

Then, finally, he clicked 'NEPO'.

This is what he found.

URGENT
FOR YOUR EYES ONLY

FILE REFERENCE: XENON/CRUISER/STIG

TOP LINE

The whole world may be in grave and present danger. As HQ of the Cruiser Corporation, the town of Bunsfold certainly is.

BACKGROUND

The Corporation has succeeded in developing computer software of such potency that it poses a global threat to society. Its first deployment is in a computer game known as Xenon. This we have seen at first hand.

Once exposed, any player will shortly forgo all other activities, spending their life staring at a screen and scarcely responding to human contact. Once the player is addicted, hidden messages are buried within the game. The recipient is powerless to resist.

The objective is manipulation. Once exposed, a subject can be told, or sold, anything – even one of those ridiculous Vauxhall Cavalier convertible conversions from years ago. Seriously, that actually happened. Total mind control.

***Only those who have not played Xenon are able to resist** – they and the mysterious operative known only as **The Stig** (refer file ref. ST888&B) – the one entity known to be immune to all forms of mind control.*

The reason for his immunity remains unknown, as his true identity remains a secret. All we know is that he turns up when we're in big trouble. Oh – and, for reasons unknown, the evil Cruiser Corporation have a bit of a thing about him.

Suddenly there was interference on the screen. The document began to blur and fade in and out of view, with only tantalising glimpses visible.

. . . hidden identity . . . ultimate weapon . . . threat to . . . extreme prejudice . . .

And then one final word.

DEATHBOT.

Minnie leaned over and shut the screen down instantly.

Ford and Sam each gave her a quizzical look.

'They were tracking us,' she explained. 'I think we got out just in time.'

The three of them sat for a moment, trying to drink it all in.

It was Minnie that broke the silence.

'Deathbot,' she said. 'Well, that doesn't sound good.'

TWENTIETH

In which Buster Mustang gets a cellmate

At the first sound of the door code being punched in, Buster opened one eye then sat bolt upright, listening hard.

Focus! What are the last two numbers?

Beep-ba-ba-beep-ba . . . short pause . . . beep-ba-beep beep beep baa.

Zero-seven-one-two-one . . . pause . . . eight-seven-nine-six . . . three-eight.

Three-eight! So now he had it. He scratched the numbers quickly into the soft plaster behind his mattress.

The entire door code.

Eleven numbers. Like his dad's cellphone. He wondered if he'd ever be calling that again to say, 'Hey, Pops, come pick me up. Sorry so late.' The thought of his father's fate made him so mad he felt the red mist ready to descend. He shook his head. Keep calm, Buster. Focus.

The door slid open. More hard-boiled eggs? Mr Cruiser, you spoil me.

But today it wasn't breakfast. Today he had a visitor.

Into the small room stooped someone he remembered well from his brief couple of weeks at Bunsfold High.

The *Head*? thought Buster. Well, I'll be . . .

'Afraid you're sharing, Mr Headmaster, sir,' said Maurice Marina, with the excess politeness that so many adults who *hadn't exactly shone* at school feel in the presence of a headmaster.

The door slammed shut. The Head stood there, taking in the scene. He looked dazed. A room about half the size of his office, where only recently he'd warned Sam Wheeler and his friends that a *storm was coming*. Had he said too much? Only by about ninety-nine per cent, he calculated. Mental note.

Boy and headmaster looked each other up and down, then shook hands, firmly.

'So you're alive, Mustang,' said the Head. 'Thank God for that, at least. Have they hurt you?'

'It's kinda the other way round, sir,' said Buster. 'I think they're hurt I won't play their game. So they got you too, huh?'

'It would seem so, er . . . Virgil, isn't it?'

'Let's . . . just stick to Mustang, thanks, sir,' replied Buster rather quickly. 'Or some people call me Buster.'

'Well, yes, Buster, they got me too. I remember a tall dark creature that seemed interested in the contents of my mind – the thoughts, the fears, the all-time favourite *University Challenge* contestant. And then it all goes blank, pretty much until I ended up being shown here to my . . . to our . . . quarters. Sorry to put you out.'

'No sweat. I'll shift my things over to this side and . . .'

Buster picked up sheets and pillows and threw them both in one fluid and painstakingly planned movement. The first towards the washbasin, the second over the dull red eye in the top corner of the cell. He looked to check: both cameras covered.

He beckoned his new cellmate close and whispered, 'We have eighty-eight seconds before they'll come in and clear the cameras. How are my folks? Still hooked on that damn game? Or doin' all they can to spring me outta here?'

'Hard to tell,' whispered the Head, picking up straight away on the fast-whispering thing. 'Your parents were posted straight back to the USA and things went strangely quiet. I began to suspect the Cruiser Corporation was more advanced in mind control than I'd realised, and even better connected. So I investigated. And, next thing I know, we're sharing a sink. As far as I can tell, there are about fifty other cells available, but they're playing the old "put them in together and eavesdrop" card. So we'll have to watch what we say.'

Buster looked crestfallen. The Head continued, still whispering, 'Listen, don't worry. If they wanted us both gone, we wouldn't be having this conversation. I think we're safe for now.' He broke off and examined the room. 'Have you learned anything we can use?'

'Xenon. It's addictive. A mind-control device that turns anyone who plays it into a slave to the Cruiser Corporation. First Bunsfold, then the world. My parents were in the first test group, and pretty soon stopped caring about much else. That's why I came here to investigate, and ended up in this cell. It's ready to be launched on the whole world, and they're expecting *everyone* will become addicted . . .'

Suddenly, a familiar voice interrupted him over the cell intercom.

'Oh, I'm not expecting it, Mr Mustang. I'm observing it.'

Buster and the headmaster looked at each other, startled.

The headmaster, looking quietly angry, pulled himself up to his full height and adopted full Headmaster Tone.

'Mr Cruiser, you're insane. Do you seriously believe one crazy billionaire –'

'Dillionaire.'

'– could ever subjugate the whole human race? With a silly *computer game?*'

'Headmaster! Welcome!' said the voice. 'I have some bad news and some very bad news. The bad news is that I have decided to give you twenty-four hours to live . . .'

There was a pause for a moment. Boy and headmaster looked at each other, shocked.

'The very bad news is that I decided this yesterday.'

Buster jumped across the cell and hit the REPLY button.

'No, no, Mr Cruiser . . . sir. If your reputation is correct, you're a man of wisdom as well as humongous intelligence. The headmaster meant no disrespect and could be a useful source of intelligence. I mean, he's a headmaster, and they pretty much know everything, right?'

Silence. Buster went on.

'Are we agreed? Over.'

There was a pause on the other end. Then . . .

'Over what?'

There was a muffled sound of the voice talking to someone. 'Maurice . . . what does he mean, "over"? Over who? How do I turn this off . . . ?'

Then, after some more muffled voices and another pause, 'Very well. We shall spare him for today. The piranha fish will be disappointed.'

The headmaster went pale and gripped the edge of the bed.

'But kindly reassure him that the entire world is indeed about to be subjugated by a *"silly computer game"*. And that as of precisely 5 p.m. on Saturday afternoon – that's twelve noon Eastern Time . . . pretty much everybody everywhere will be working for . . . The Man!'

He paused for a moment.

'And The Man's name is . . . Me!'

TWENTY-FIRST

*In which Sam contemplates getting back
on two wheels, and the plight of a scruffy
labradoodle makes the decision easier*

Sam awoke in good spirits as usual. He was a morning person, and the first thirty seconds of the new day were just dandy. Then he remembered where he was, everything that had happened and the gathering storm – at which point his morale collapsed faster than a paper umbrella in the shower.

No porridge for breakfast, which he didn't miss, but also no 'have a good day, darling', which he did. Just two dead-eyed parents, looking as if they hadn't slept in a week. Sam stuffed the last two spoonfuls of cereal into his sinking stomach, grabbed his schoolbag and trudged out of the front door. But before reaching the garden gate he turned right and walked slowly towards the tatty garage at the side of his house.

After a moment's pause, he hoisted up the garage's rollover door and stood silently frowning at a grubby, dented BMX bike tucked in the corner.

He gently hoisted the bike out into the sunlight.

They say everyone is born with one special talent. And though he was pants at maths and the worst goalkeeper in the history of his previous school, one thing was clear.

Despite what the Cruiser Crew believed, Sam Wheeler could ride a bike just fine. And he had the medals to prove it.

But he hadn't sat on one for months. Not since the accident.

He balanced the BMX in his hands. There was nothing flash about it. Its tech spec was light years behind Cabriola Cruiser's. Then again, everything was.

Didn't matter to him though. Because this bike had something more important.

When it turned out he had a talent for riding, his mum had saved for months to buy the perfect bike he'd assembled in his head. Every component had been exhaustively lightened and strengthened, everything unnecessary deleted and every element designed to mesh together like a watch mechanism.

After months of neglect it looked a bit of a state, but as Sam held it, the bike twitched. Like a wand reunited with a boy wizard, it was alive again. Sure, it didn't have tech. But it had soul.

But as he rolled the handlebar grips lightly in each palm, something he'd been burying for months shot back into his head. Just as he knew it would.

Screeching tyres. Shouting. Gramps tumbling to push him from the path of the white van. Then the stomach-turning sight of his grandfather lying deathly pale across the middle of the road, blood pouring from where the wing mirror had cracked his head.

It had all been Sam's fault. And he'd sworn he wouldn't sit

on a saddle again until Gramps was back home and recovered.

Now he was, but Sam still wasn't ready. Not even close.

He set the bike back against the side of the garage, pulled the door down behind him and trudged off, head bowed, towards school.

With no interruptions from Minnie, Ford or Dennis Charade this time, he was ahead of schedule. He headed towards the park to kill some time.

As he sat on the bench, he was jolted by something cold thrusting itself into his hand. Something cold, small and wet.

It was a black nose that looked exactly like an olive. And it was attached to a sorry-looking brown mongrel with a white flash on its forehead.

'TG!' he yelped, thrilled to see the shaggy mutt still at large. Two mournful brown eyes stared up at him, and a twig-matted tail managed a single sorry wag.

The dog walked slowly round the bench, and it was only then that Sam saw how badly it was injured. It limped back towards him whimpering softly, clearly protecting its front leg, and collapsed on the ground by Sam's feet.

'Here, boy. Don't worry, I'm here now. And I'm going to get you sorted,' he said calmly, trying not to sound as upset as he really was. Who would do something like that to a dog?

TG rested its head on Sam's trainers. Sam saw something stuck in its neck, held in place by his collar.

It was a dull, black metallic shape, like a finger. Sam gently removed it from the poor dog's neck and held it up to the sky.

Metal. Light, but exceptionally strong. It looked familiar . . . and, when it suddenly grew an edge so sharp he couldn't hold on to it, he realised. Between clenched teeth, he muttered its name.

'Narnium.'

TWENTY-SECOND

**In which it all gets WAY too exciting to waste
time telling you about it up here**

Sam Wheeler had to think fast. He had ninety-nine problems, and a dog was one.

First job was to get TG to safety – and the clock was against him. BCHQ was out. He'd never make it back in time, even assuming he could find it on his own. No, home was the only option. Sure, he'd miss assembly, but he could still get there for his first lesson.

Problem Number Two was that his mum was sneezingly allergic to dogs. So while he coaxed (and, for the final stretch, carried) the injured mutt back towards home, he improvised a plan. He'd have to rope in Gramps to provide first aid until he could get back from school. Luckily, the old boy could never resist a pooch in need.

Sure enough, after listening to Sam's garbled explanation, Gramps swept TG up and headed straight towards the garage. 'I'll have her fed, watered and rested up by the time you're back.'

'Her?' said Sam.

'Yup,' said Gramps, with a wink. 'It's a girl. Remind me not to recommend "vet" as your career.' He got to work, examining a deep cut just under the dog's foreleg. 'Nasty. Looks like someone meant to hurt her. Now, you get off to school. We'll talk about this tonight.'

That just left Problem Number Three: how to deal with his buddies from the Cruiser Crew.

But as he got to the school gate he found Ford Harrison waiting for him, looking serious.

'School not started yet?' he asked.

'Nope. Twenty-minute delay while the cops talk to the staff about the Head,' said Ford. He looked left and right, then lowered his voice. 'They left his study unlocked, so it was the perfect time to nip in and have a nose around.'

'You snuck into the Head's office?' said Sam.

'They haven't combed it for clues yet,' said Ford. 'And if there's anything to be found, I'd rather we got to it before Mr Plod. Bunsfold's Finest are a little too close to the Cruiser Corporation for my liking. Anyway, I found something. Stuffed under the cushion of his chair.'

'What?' said Sam, a bit anxiously.

Ford hesitated. Sam had never seen him this jumpy.

'Three scribbled words.' He paused for a moment. 'DEATHBOT. SAVE YOURSELVES.'

'Blimey,' said Sam. 'Him again.'

'It gets worse,' said Ford.

Once again he glanced sideways, then signalled for Sam to

follow him away from some kids standing nearby with their noses stuffed in a Xenon game.

He stared hard at Sam. 'The note was addressed to . . . us.'

'*What?*' said Sam. 'DEATHBOT. SAVE YOURSELVES – and he sent it to *us*?'

'Yup. You and me, Wheels. Just you and me.'

'Not Minnie?'

'Nope. Thankfully,' said Ford with feeling, bristling like a protective knight in shining armour.

'Well, that's something. Let's go and tell her,' said Sam.

'You won't need to,' said Ford. 'She knows. Everyone does. I put the note back, and Hornet found it. Then some kids overheard him discussing it with the police, and word's got out.' He paused again. 'But that's not all. Mr Leyland hadn't finished writing. Someone – something – got to him first.'

For the second time since he'd arrived in Bunsfold, Sam was rattled. But, just when the last thing he needed was a reminder of the first time, he saw the Cruiser Crew.

A kerfuffle. Raised voices. They had their latest victim surrounded against the science-block wall.

Sam set off towards them at speed.

'Uh-oh,' said Ford, watching him stride away. 'Loose cannon on deck.'

He winced as the giant, hooded Hummer immediately swivelled to meet Sam. As he had the turning circle of the stretch-limo version of a real Hummer, this took longer than you'd think.

'Hold it right there, Hippy Hair. This doesn't concern you,' he said, in his horror-movie-trailer voice. 'This is C-Crew business.'

'Shut up, Hummer,' said Sam. 'I'm not in the mood.'

The hooded henchman took a few more lumbering steps and the boys could finally see what was going on behind. It wasn't quite what they'd expected.

Cabriola Cruiser – who always looked as if she knew something everybody else didn't – was standing face to face with an angry Minnie Cooper.

But it turned out it was Minnie who was doing the interrogating.

Cabriola hissed something under her breath that Sam couldn't quite make out, though he thought he'd heard the word 'Deathbot' in there somewhere. Minnie was looking at her furiously, her huge dark eyes wider than ever.

Sam and Ford stepped straight up to Cabriola. 'Pick on her, Cruiser, and you pick on us.'

Cabriola turned to them with a half-smile. 'Check out your bodyguard detail, Minnie. One tiny loser who can't talk to you without turning beetroot and a long-haired speccy new kid who can't ride a bike. Get back on your tricycle and ride out of town, cowboy. Remember . . . Deathbot's coming to get ya!'

Sam said nothing. But inside, something was boiling up.

Cabriola caught his expression and sensed blood in the water.

'Want to teach me a lesson, new kid? I can see you're dying

to. Ready to take that challenge after all? Charade has a bike here ready and waiting for you.'

And, hearing his cue, her weasely trainee henchman quickly dismounted and pushed his ride towards Sam.

Sam twitched. His right hand shot out to grab the handlebar. But then stopped just short.

Cue sarcastic encouragement from the Crew.

'Woohoo! C'mon, Speccy . . . You can do it!'

Sam stopped himself, and breathed deeply – just like Gramps had taught him to do before a race – until the anger started to subside. If he was going to take this bully down, it wasn't going to be like this. Not here. Not on her terms.

'What is it, new kid?' said Spooner. 'Oh, now get me less. Tum other sime?'

'Yes,' said Sam. 'Some other time.'

'Don't worry. I found some stabilisers on the internet. I'll lend you the sink!'

As the laughter rose, Minnie stepped in. Good old Minnie.

'Spooner! Cabriola!' she called, and every head turned. 'Leave him ALONE, for heaven's sake. There are more important things going on around here. Now . . . are you telling me that's really *everything* you know? About the Deathbot?'

Before Bunsfold's bully-in-residence could answer, the bell went for assembly and anxious teachers thundered across the playground, rounding up kids.

Minnie gestured to Sam and Ford to follow her round the back of the dining hall. She sat down against the wall.

Assembly could wait. This was serious.

'Did you find anything out?' said Ford.

Minnie looked at him solemnly. 'Not much. Not from her, anyway. Swears she knows next to nothing. But some of the kids overheard the cops talking, and . . .'

'And?'

'Look. It's just scraps. Chinese whispers. No one knows if the Deathbot really exists. Some say it's just a rumour the Cruiser Corp has spread to put the wind up their rivals.'

'Okay. But what is it meant to be, exactly?'

Minnie stared hard at them before replying.

'It's supposed to be the ultimate weapon. A drone robot designed not only to kill, but to terrify.'

Ford gulped. 'How?'

'Gets all available data on you and scans it to find your deepest fear. Then brainwashes you into thinking that's exactly what it is.'

'Cobblers,' said Sam, looking increasingly unconvinced. 'This all sounds nuts to me. I think someone's messing with our heads.' And he glanced up towards the mansion on the hill. 'And I know who.'

Ford was puzzled. 'Talk me through that again,' he said to Minnie.

'Look, what are you most scared of?' asked Minnie.

'Flesh-eating zombie,' said Ford.

Minnie turned to Sam.

'What about you? What's your deepest, darkest fear?'

'Mr Rodius's bottom,' he replied. 'I'd like to see the Deathbot turn itself into *that*.'

Minnie stared at him for a moment. Then smiled.

Sam went on. 'Okay. Enough already. I think it's time to blow the whistle and tell the adults everything we know. I'm taking this all the way to the top.'

'But the headmaster's gone, remember?' said Ford.

'Oh yeah,' replied Sam. 'All right, I'm taking this all the way to the middle. Where's Hornet when you actually need him?'

'No!' said Minnie. 'Don't do that, Wheels. I mean it.'

'She's right,' said Ford. 'We've no idea who we can trust.'

'Then what *do* we do?'

Minnie looked at him hard. Then, after a pause, 'It's simple,' she said. 'We have to find The Stig.'

TWENTY-THIRD

**In which we find out lots we really didn't
want to know about the Deathbot, and Cbrla's
mssgng styl gts vn mr annyng**

That afternoon, at precisely 3.55, Maurice Marina entered
MOTH's cavernous Surveillance Hall.

''Scuse me, boss,' he coughed.

Cruiser sighed. 'What is it, Maurice?'

'It's the Chamber. Of Combustion. It's making funny
noises. Getting ever so hot. Nearly boilin' over. And you said if
it ever did, there'd be an apoc . . . apoc . . .'

'Apocalyptic nuclear meltdown that could plunge Surrey
into darkness for a hundred years, yes – and? Can't you see I'm
busy? That Harrison boy is about to cycle home from school,
and I need to track him. I'm beginning to suspect he's not as
stupid as he looks.'

'Oh yeah. And the atomic reactor's gone a bit ballistic 'n'
all.'

'Well, you can never trust an atom, Maurice. They make
up everything.'

Having heard the joke several hundred times before,
Maurice wasn't smiling.

PT continued. 'All right. So pop down to North Korea and pick up some more fusion coolant.'

'Sure, boss. It'll cost a few million though.'

'Well, get it from the change jar by the back door on your way out. Now be gone! I'm busy!'

PT Cruiser reclined extravagantly in his unicorn-leather armchair and sighed. There was still so much to *do*. One lifetime, he had concluded, was simply not enough.

It was 3.58 p.m. Time to activate Surveillance Camera 877B. Location: a black rubbish bin at the edge of the Bunsfold Recreation Ground.

From here he could track this afternoon's subject. An intensely meddlesome boy called Harrison.

And, sure enough, there he was: caught on camera sedately pedalling a sit-up-and-beg bicycle along the cycle path bordering the park.

The dillionaire smiled to himself. 'Ha! Finding things a little . . . *hotter* now, are we, Master Harrison? Or should I say . . . Corporal Slow?' And he waited for Ford to cycle out of camera range.

And waited.

Aaaaand waited.

Until, finally, Ford disappear— Oh. No. Still going.

This was taking more time than he'd thought. PT's formidable four-figure IQ calculated that by the time the meddling boy had finally pedalled out of view, his mobile phone would be obsolete.

Patience, PT. Patience.

Maurice's news about the Chamber of Combustion had confirmed his suspicions. His white-suited nemesis was near.

Yes. *Him.*

The Stig.

He could feel his presence – even, sometimes, sniff a whiff of hot buttered clutch on the breeze.

Now the issue was beyond all doubt. The Cruiser Corporation's all-sensing surveillance infrastructure had detected more tiny V8-shaped blips in the space–time continuum.

More intriguingly still, each detection had been recorded in the vicinity of two unusually irritating Bunsfold High children.

Ford Harrison. And Sam Wheeler.

But what connected these two piles of profoundly unpromising genetic material to his mighty White Nemesis? Was The Stig protecting them? Stalking them? Making little models of them to give away with petrol?

Further investigation was required. As PT always liked to say, time spent in surveillance is rarely wasted. But strangely – and suspiciously – on this occasion, his data room was of little use.

It seemed that, along with the Mustang boy and Minnie Cooper, these pests were the last children in Bunsfold to resist the irresistible addiction of Xenon. With no gaming data to analyse, he was in the dark. The one place PT Cruiser hated being.

Once again he scoured Sam Wheeler's wafer-thin file for any teensy hint, trick or cheat to get him to the next level – a clue as to why The Stig would meddle in his itty-bitty life. But even with Deathbot activated at Level 28 Surveillance Mode, pickings were still strangely thin.

Though it *had* transpired that the Wheeler boy was a rather more accomplished cyclist than he was prepared to let on.

This last point unsettled PT. I mean, if you've got it, why not flaunt it? He couldn't understand it. And as he always said . . . if you don't understand it, get rid of it.

Just then, the eyes on his Daughter app flashed white.

Tsk. More interruptions. Their next interaction wasn't due for eight days. Let's get this over with.

PT:	Cbrla. I'm bsy wth my wrk.
Cabriola:	Dd. We need 2 talk.
PT:	I've told U. Stop calling me Dd. It's creepy.
Cabriola:	Not til U tell me wt I need 2 know. PapaBear.
PT:	Aaaaaargh!

Pause. Then:

PT:	What is the nature of your enquiry? Press one for 'pocket money', two for
Cabriola:	Wt is the Deathbot??

Long pause. Then:

PT:	There's no one available to take your call right

now. At the tone, please leave your name + a short message +

Cabriola: I'm serious. Wt is the Deathbot?

Another long pause. Then:

PT: Why? Have you seen him too?

Cabriola: Not persnlly. But apprntly he's roaming around Bnsfld Woods at night abducting headmasters. And wt with U being the only artificial intelligence dillionaire in Bnsfld, natrlly ppl r looking at me. I cant believe U wd do nythng so mbrrssng in frnt of all my friends!

PT: Deny everything. Works 4 me.

Cabriola: Whatevs. Now WT, xctly, is this Deathbot thing?!!

PT: Hang on, I'm switching 2 Dictate mode for this. 2 exciting. Hng on . . . Okay. I'm really glad you asked. Showing an interest in my work at last. So. Deathbot is just something I threw together a few months back. Sort of a prototype really. I was kicking the tyres, pushing the envelope on a few pieces of new Cruiser tech and I threw them together in a hurry and, well, he came out a little . . . wrong.

Cabriola: Wt do U mean, wrong?

PT: Well . . . sort of hideously evil.

Cabriola: ????!!!!

PT: But cute as well, you know? I mean he's bad beyond any human imagining, sure, but charming too – a real chip off the old block actually. On the first morning he was activated I came down to breakfast and I couldn't find him anywhere, and then I catch him hiding behind the sofa looking really sick and turns out he's eaten his way through a whole pack of scientists!

Cabriola: Scntsts??

PT: Yes! The guys that built him in the lab! I mean, he didn't own up or anything, but they'd all disappeared and he had little bits of lab coat all around his mouth so of course I knew it was him. I had to tell him off but he looked so adorable I could hardly keep a straight face.

Cabriola: U created a rbt that's evil?!

PT: Well, I prefer 'high-spirited'. But I mean, what can you do? That's kids these days. But he had real talent too, I think. Apparently he got one of those scientists to eat himself. Just by talking to him. I mean, persuading someone to eat themselves, that's not easy to do, you know? I tried it once and the guy just looked at me like I was mad.

Cabriola: Wt n earth have U bn doing! U prmsd me U wr only making computr gms & the VV occasional nuclear warhead.

| **PT:** | Well, strictly speaking that's true. But . . . the Company's Black Ops Division does make some other things too . . . |
| **Cabriola:** | ???????? |

Pause.

PT:	Oh for heaven's sake all right. I know I'm going to regret telling you this, but, well, 'Papa Bear' builds a lot of indescribably destructive robotic weapons for evil foreign powers. There. I've said it. And I don't want you posting that anywhere.
Cabriola:	But Y wd NE1 want an evil rbt?
PT:	Sigh. Very well. Let me explain. Here at the Cruiser Corporation we always put our customers first. So, every few months I try to get around to see them and the feedback this year was yes, sure, Cruiser drone robots are really good at killing people and totally reliable and economical to run yadda yadda. But you know what, PT? they said. They're just not that scary.
Cabriola:	????????
PT:	So, anyway, this one morning I'm sitting there with my protein shake and I'm looking at last night's Xenon data, which tells me everything about anyone who ever plays it, and I'm thinking how cool it is that it goes right into a dude's head and finds out

	everything – including the one thing that really freaks them out, right? That's absolutely guaranteed to give them an instant pant – sorry, trouser – accident?
Cabriola:	MY DAD IS CRIMINALLY INSANE 😳
PT:	So then I'm looking at Narnium, which can change its molecular structure into any form, and suddenly I'm wondering – hey! Why not put the two together, and make an indescribably clever and evil killer robot that both knows what really scares you and then turns himself into it! I mean, how sick would that be?
Cabriola:	V sick ndeed. Wt duz he look like & where is he now?
PT:	Dark. 7ft tall. Black visor. Can't miss him. Though of course he can change shape if he needs to. Might be pretending. As for where he is right now? Out on a mission, looking for something I greatly desire to possess.
Cabriola:	Wt else could U pssbly want?

Pause.

PT:	There is no one available to take your call. Please leave a
Cabriola:	Wait a minute . . . This isn't smthng 2 do wth tht white-suited weirdo in the wds, is it?

Longer pause. Before:

PT:	Might be.
Cabriola:	It is, isn't it! I NU it! Who is he NEway? A rcng drvr?
PT:	Not *a* racing driver. *The* Racing Driver.
Cabriola:	Well, I think U got sm kind of hopeless man-crush on hm.
PT:	Have not.
Cabriola:	Hv.
PT:	Have not so. Hey – talk to the screen. I have work to do. Skedaddle!

And with that PT flicked off the Chat app, reclined in his armchair and resumed observation of the meddlesome Ford Harrison. The very boy, it transpired, who had recently shoved a stuffed meerkat right up Surveillance Camera 788C.

Time for some payback. And, for Evil Gaming Genius PT Cruiser, revenge was a dish best eaten hot.

TWENTY-FOURTH

In which Buster goes on a reconnaissance mission

Thump, bounce, thud.

Thump, bounce, thud.

Thump, bounce, thud.

The baseball ricocheted off Buster's cell wall and hurtled into his glove.

He exchanged a fleeting glance with the headmaster. Okay, he was ready. Time to initiate Plan Finding Out Stuff.

He reached for the cell-intercom button.

'Hey, fellas. I have a request this morning.'

'What.'

'Tell your boss I have something to tell him. In person.'

There was a gale of rumbling laughter. 'In person? Ha! Good luck with that.'

Buster went on.

'Tell him it concerns . . . The Stig.'

Instantly, the laughter stopped.

Precisely one second later PT Cruiser was on the line.

'What do you know?' he said flatly.

'I have information. About the man you know as . . . The Stig.'

'So he's a *man*? Ha! I knew it. I just *knew* it. Maurice reckoned –'

Buster interrupted him. 'Maybe. But you're only gonna hear it in person. I've got the juice on this guy and, if you want it, I'm trading. But I want fresh air and a view. So it's your place, not mine.'

Long pause. PT continued.

'Very well.'

'Roger that,' replied Buster.

There was a brief pause, then vague sounds of talking at the other end. 'Maurice . . . who on earth is Roger That? Fetch me any data we have on a Roger That. What? Well, he's got a stupid second name, I'll tell you that for nothing. How do I turn this thing off . . . ?'

Buster and the Head glanced at each other knowingly. So far, so good.

It had been the headmaster's idea. A last throw of the dice. The killer robot that had first abducted Buster (it all seemed so very long ago now) had asked just one question.

'WHERE IS THE STIG?'

And, just as he'd hoped, the simple act of dangling the same name was about to get him some of the only currency that counted in MOTH.

Knowledge.

Buster composed himself. What he and the headmaster really knew about The Stig could be written on the back of a postage stamp with a fat pen. But, hey, details. He'd improvise.

Moments later, familiar footsteps shuffled up to the door.

Beep-ba-ba-beep-ba . . . short pause . . . beep-ba-beep beep beep baa.

Maurice Marina arrived, silently tied a blindfold over Buster's eyes and led him out of the cell.

The boy breathed deeply. Fresh air! He felt almost light-headed.

Focus, Buster. This was a one-shot deal.

They walked up to what felt like a – golf buggy? Airport luggage cart? The buzzy engine started immediately and they were on the move. They bumped on to what felt like a rough, grassy surface. Buggy, definitely. He listened carefully for clues to where he was going. He'd seen it done in a film.

At thirty-seven seconds, to the left what sounded like a . . . Nah. But it did sound *exactly* like one.

'Is that a *bear*?' he asked his escort.

'Nope,' said Maurice Marina. 'It's a pair of bears. Doesn't do to get too close. I mean, it's a deep pit and everything – don't get me wrong – but they can swipe pretty high when they ain't eaten for a week. That's what separates the dillionaires from the billionaires. Detail. Excuse me.'

Buster heard a walkie-talkie crackle into life.

'Marina to Drawbridge. Incoming. Over.'

'Reading you, Marina. Lowering in . . . five, four, three, two, one . . .'

'Toxic sludge is lookin' especially radioactive today,' said Maurice. 'You'd come out glowin'. Like that five-eyed hedgehog we fished out last week.'

'That's what I'm here for,' said the drawbridge guy. 'So you don't have to wade across. Heeeeere's Bridget . . .'

Buster heard the clunk of something heavy being lowered into position by clanking great chains – and then Maurice's voice again.

'Put your hand up, kid. Gentle like. Careful! Feel that?'

Buster felt metal at arm's length above his head.

'Sharpest portcullis in Surrey,' said Maurice proudly. 'Detail again, see? Now we walk the last bit. Past the . . . Afternoon, Sergei. Lovely day for it. Fish hungry?'

'Always,' said a second voice.

To his right, quite close, Buster heard a splashing, gnashing sound. The scent of blood. Then sploshes. It sounded like limbs being dropped into a tank . . . Nah, couldn't be.

A little way off he heard a highly tuned two-stroke engine near the rev limit. The smell of hot brakes, rubber and a warm track. Go-karts! Fast ones. Really fast ones.

He made a mental note of it all. One day he'd have to navigate his way through this crazy mansion to get to the one part he'd really need to find. The place he'd calculated he'd be taken to now.

PT's lair. Mission Control.

Finally they stopped. Okay, Buster, wait for it. Here it comes.

Beep-ba-ba-beep-ba . . . short pause . . . beep-ba-beep beep beep baa.

There it is, right there, thought Buster. *THE CODE. MUST REMEMBER THE CODE.*

Off came the blindfold.

Finally he was face to face with his jailer.

TWENTY-FIFTH

In which cat meets mouse. But which is which?

Standing stock still in the middle of the room was a short, bald beardy guy. And he was wearing a black – was that a *onesie*?

Was *this* the boss man on the other end of the mic? The Wizard of Oz, the Mastermind Behind, and almost certainly the only billionaire in the whole village?

Meanwhile, in his head, Buster was silently chanting the door code over and over.

Beep-ba-ba-beep-ba . . . short pause . . . beep-ba-beep beep beep baa.

Cruiser said nothing. Buster broke the ice.

'So. Dr Cruiser, I presume.'

The beardy figure smiled.

'So. Buster Mustard. We meet at last.' And he paused for a moment. 'But then I feel I know you already.'

Buster looked around. 'So this is where it all happens, huh? The mythical lair. The room they say you never leave.'

PT smiled.

'Oh, there's no need to leave.' He cast his arm across the innumerable screens covering the far wall. 'There's a great big world in here.'

Buster glanced around surreptitiously.

One basketball hoop attached to the wall. One untouched basketball still in its wrapper. One leather armchair. One opened box of Wagon Wheels.

And that was pretty much it . . . No, wait.

To the left of the armchair. A single row of four giant electrical plugs stuck into bucket-sized sockets, each labelled with a big red sticker.

The first one read HOT WATER.

The second, PIRANHA TANK LIGHTING.

The third, GLOBAL XENON SUPERBRAIN (SUBJUGATION OF MANKIND).

And the fourth, KETTLE.

Buster had a passing suspicion that at least one of those might come in useful down the line.

If he fancied a shower, say.

PT noticed him looking.

'I see you're admiring my giant plugs.'

'They're hard to miss. What's that all about?'

'Power, Mr Mustang.' He put his fingers together for a moment. 'Allow me to provide a brief demonstration.'

PT leaned over and, with great deliberation, pulled the plug labelled PIRANHA TANK LIGHTING out of the wall.

Deep under their feet, Buster heard dull and distant thudding.

'That, Mr Mustang, is the sound of several hundred carnivorous fish bumping into each other.'

He looked at Buster triumphantly, his eyes shining.

'As I said. Power.'

'That reminds me,' said Buster. 'Where in the States are you from? Your accent seems a little . . . inconsistent.'

PT looked momentarily flustered. 'I'll ask the questions,' he said as he struggled to lift the giant plug back into its socket.

Then Buster spotted them. Hurriedly hidden in a corner, seven or eight life-size cut-outs of what looked like a . . . racing driver in a white suit?

Bingo. That *must* be him. Exactly as the Head had described.

'I see you've surrounded yourself with life-size cut-outs of The Stig,' said Buster.

At the very mention of the S-word, PT jumped up from behind the armchair, still wrestling with the giant plug. When he spoke, his voice was almost a whisper.

'What do you know?' he asked.

'Pictures of him everywhere, huh? What is it, some sort of hopeless man-crush?'

'What the . . . ? What do you . . . ? What are you suggesting, exactly . . . ?' spluttered PT. 'The Stig is my nemesis,' he said firmly. 'And *nothing* more.'

'If you say so. And if he's your nemesis, I'm guessing you plan to destroy him, right? But how, exactly?'

'Well, I'm glad you asked me tha—' The dillionaire stopped himself. 'Hmm. Clever boy. Goading me into revealing my plan.' He paused again, deep in thought.

'Very well. Your fate is sealed in any case. I may as well share all with you. Some would call it breathtaking complacency, but hey, I'm on a roll here. You asked me how I plan to destroy The Stig. Behold!'

PT reached down and pulled a concealed lever by his chair.

Instantly the black wall to his right slid upwards, revealing a giant cylindrical mechanism breathtaking in its scope and majesty.

Once more, PT surveyed his deadly motorised masterpiece with awe. For here (still) towered the Engine from the End of the World: the nightmarish Chamber of Combustion. In the dark red light of the chamber, PT Cruiser seemed even more insane than usual.

'Feel that, boy? POWERRRRRRRRRRRRRR!'

Buster shrugged. 'Okay, I get it. A giant engine to destroy a racing driver. But how will you catch him?'

Before PT could answer, a penny dropped.

'The kart race!' said Buster. 'The one you're all preparing for! I hear about it every time your goons walk me around this hell hole. It's all about catching The Stig, isn't it?'

'Hell hole? You really think? I was going for *studious menace*. It's funny . . . You have one thing in your own head, and people –'

'Okay. So how does it all play out?'

PT took a deep breath and leaned back in his armchair.

'The Stig is unknowable in every regard bar this,' he said. 'He exists for only two things. First, to race. Second, to very occasionally turn up and save mankind from tyranny.'

He paused.

'But, of those two, racing's way out front.'

Maurice quietly put on his headphones.

PT went on. 'So I have set up a lure so fiendish that the word "trap" does not begin to cover it. First, the irresistible challenge of a race he cannot possibly win against overwhelmingly superior opposition: me. Second, the simultaneous global launch of a mind-controlling computer game that will subjugate mankind. The perfect carrot; the perfect stick.'

He paused, deep in contemplation. 'In fact, the whole race is one huge carrot stick.'

Buster grimaced. 'And me?'

'Oh, don't worry, Mr Mustang. Rest assured you'll have a ringside seat. A little too close for comfort, I fear.'

'One more question,' said Buster. 'Why?'

PT Cruiser looked stumped. 'Why what?'

'Why global domination? Why enslave the human race? Why go to all this trouble just to nobble a racing driver? I mean, how much more power and wealth could a tech dillionaire possibly need?'

'Power and wealth?' said PT. 'It's true – I've had my share. And yours too. But that's not the point. You see, Mr Mustard, beneath all *this* –' and he swished an arm all around himself – 'the signature black onesie, the four-figure IQ, the dillions safely tucked up in easily the biggest savings account at Bunsfold Post Office. Not to mention a genius with technology beyond any mortal comprehension . . .'

Maurice yawned.

' . . . beneath all this lies the simple beating heart of . . . a gamer. Yes, the world is simply another game to me. And Xenon takes me to the next level.'

Boy and man stood facing one another in silence as, far beneath them, the sloppy thud of crashing piranha fish beat on.

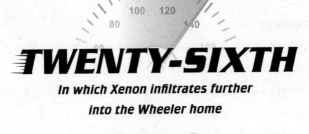

TWENTY-SIXTH

In which Xenon infiltrates further
into the Wheeler home

When another interminable afternoon at Bunsfold High finally drew to a close, Sam asked Minnie if he could walk her home after school.

'Kind, but I'll pass, thanks,' she said instantly. 'My dad's got builders in and the whole place is a shambles.'

'You sure? I mean, you're my best mate in Bunsfold and I just thought it would be cool to check out your crib and meet your folks 'n' all.'

'Trust me,' said Minnie flatly. 'You're not missing much.'

Sam continued, tentatively. 'Cooper, is everything, you know, okay at home? You never really talk about it, and I wondered . . .' His voice trailed away.

Minnie sighed. 'All right. Here's the scoop. I don't know my mum. She left just after I was born. And my dad's an idiot and a bully.' She paused for a moment. 'There. I said it.'

Sam was taken aback. She went on. 'I think he has . . . issues. Anyway, that's all the news that's fit to print. Can we talk about something else now?'

But he wasn't letting it drop. 'What kind of issues?'

Minnie sighed.

'Standard dad stuff, only worse. Always has to know e*very single thing* I'm doing. Never asks, only tells. And believes there are only two kinds of opinion in the world – his one, and the wrong one. What can I say? He's just not a very nice man. Now can we change the subject?' Finally, that smile returned. 'But I like it that you care.'

Then she flipped things around.

'So what about you, Wheeler-Dealer? What makes you tick? Don't you ever feel like giving up on Bunsfold? I mean, we could always just play Xenon, get brainwashed and live in ignorant bliss. You know, leave it to the grown-ups to sort out all . . . *this.*'

She waved her arm at an endless traffic jam stretching all the way into Bunsfold. Roadworks blocked one side of the road. A single red-eyed builder sat on the end of his shovel staring at a Xenon console.

'It's crossed my mind,' said Sam. 'But . . . I just think we have to try. You know, not duck it, or just sit around talking about it. My grandad – you must meet him – has this saying: *Action has a magical force.* If you get up off your butt and try stuff, well, things magically start to change. And if you don't, they don't.'

He paused, and shrugged. 'Anyway, I don't want to end up some day as a bitter, disillusioned fourteen-year-old looking back on a wasted life.'

Minnie stared at him for a moment, thoughtfully. Then she

smiled. 'You're a good man, Sam Wheeler.'

So Sam invited her back to his house instead, to come and say hi to Gramps and – though he kept this part a surprise – to meet his other new best friend, a scrub-coloured mongrel with a white flash on its forehead.

When they arrived, Sam's mum was sitting in the living room with the hint of a smile. She even put down her phone and looked up when they came in. Sam's spirits instantly rose.

After introducing herself to Minnie – who was as charming as always with grown-ups – Mrs Wheeler smiled at her son. 'Now, Sam. I've got you a present. Nothing big, but I thought it might take your mind off all this other nonsense.'

She handed him a rectangular box.

Sam and Minnie froze at the word on the side.

Xenon.

'Invented right here in Bunsfold! Your dad and I just love it, and we couldn't bear to think of you missing out. A "game beyond all imagining", they call it, and how right they are. Minnie? What's your high score? Mine's –'

'Oh, games aren't really my thing, Mrs W,' said Minnie.

'They weren't mine! But I love it. Go on, Sam, try it. How lovely, to be just starting out. I promise you'll never –'

She was interrupted by the sound of the back door crashing open, and the loudest, angriest bark Sam had ever heard.

TG Dog limped into the room and crouched in the doorway, teeth bared. Mrs Wheeler screamed, grabbed Minnie and jumped back against the wall. The mongrel growled quietly and prowled painfully towards Minnie, whose face was now completely white.

'TG! Stop!' yelled Sam. He grabbed the angry pooch by the collar and yanked her backwards. 'Minnie – drop the box! It's Xenon . . . She hates it!'

But Mrs W had gripped Minnie to her in fright. The dog faced them, still growling. 'She's just trying to protect me!' said Sam. 'From the game!'

In panic, he grabbed TG by her wounded hind legs, yanked her backwards out of the room and slammed the door shut behind him. The dog yelped in agony and collapsed on the floor of the kitchen. Now she was shaking and whimpering. Sam was fighting back tears. What had he done?

At that moment, Gramps came through the back door.

'What on earth's going on in here?' He walked straight through to the living room and calmed his distraught daughter. Minnie sounded just fine. Doesn't scare easily, thought Sam again, feeling strangely proud. Then Gramps returned to the kitchen and crouched over the dog.

TG was convulsing. 'She's in shock,' he said quietly. 'Might be the wounds, might be some kind of stroke.'

'She was just trying to protect me!' said Sam, wiping his eyes forcefully.

'We've got to get to the vet,' said Gramps. And he grabbed the keys to the family's ancient Land Rover.

TWENTY-SEVENTH

It's a dog's life. Or death

Sam climbed on to the front bench seat and nursed the dog's head in his lap. The scruffy mongrel was still shaking.

'She's closed her eyes,' he cried. 'We're losing her!'

Gramps turned the ignition, cranked the engine and . . . nothing.

He turned it again.

Still nothing. Finally the starter motor wheezed agonisingly before catching and firing. Gramps revved the engine, crunched the gearbox into first gear, pulled away down the drive and turned left towards Bunsfold High Street.

Then stopped.

Gridlock.

Up ahead, a nose-to-tail traffic jam stretched as far as Sam could see.

'No!' screamed Sam. He grabbed Gramps by the shoulder. The old man turned to him. Even he looked stumped.

They sat there, stuck fast and flapping, like flies in glue.

'We're losing her,' said Sam desperately. 'We're losing TG!'

But just then something very strange began to happen.

The air was thick, and everything went suddenly quiet.

Slowly at first, but quickening, a soft breeze blew down Bunsfold High Street. A dozen car alarms went off at precisely the same moment. A cat, a dog and a squirrel huddled together under a bus shelter.

Something peculiar was stirring.

All eyes turned east, across the river.

Because far out across the fields a tiny speck was moving towards them.

And it was white.

Sam turned to Gramps, but the old man was squinting at the figure in the distance.

It was wearing a white racing suit with a dark visor.

It was . . . *him.*

The Stig marched right up to the Landie, opened the door and gestured for Gramps to move over. The old man shuffled along the bench seat next to Sam and TG.

And at that precise second, eighty-eight overstuffed black rubbish bins right across Bunsfold swivelled noiselessly to face the Land Rover.

The mute white racer fastened his seatbelt and tested the movement of the gearshift, clutch and throttle. Then he turned on the Land Rover's ancient radio and fiddled with the tuning knob until an old, crackling record came on. It was 'Yes, We Have No Bananas'.

Just for an instant the dark visor turned to Gramps, who could only stare back, mouth agape.

Then the silent driver crashed the Landie into first gear,

swung the wheel hard right and shot out of the traffic jam . . . straight into the river running next to the road.

Deeper and deeper they drove, until water was washing up over the bonnet and lapping the windscreen. But they were moving.

As soon as they'd passed the roadworks, The Stig swung the Land Rover up out of the water, flicked its transfer box into low-ratio mode and headed towards the near-vertical slope of the riverbank. The engine groaned and steamed, and the car slid backwards in the mud, wheels spinning wildly. They were sliding into the river!

The Stig seemed unconcerned. He fiddled with the radio again until he found what was looking for – a 'Teach Yourself Swahili' language lesson. Then, satisfied, he gunned the engine one more time, his feet danced on the pedals in a blur and suddenly the Landie launched itself over the brow of the hill and thumped down on the other side.

At last! They were on the main road into town, and out of traffic.

Second. Third.

Top gear.

'We have guests,' said Gramps.

Sam caught the shadow of a vehicle closing on them quickly from behind.

Then another.

He turned and saw the menacing silhouettes of two all-black Mercedes Vito vans closing fast.

A speed camera flashed as the Landie sped past, then swivelled to follow it like an insect eye on a stalk.

The first van revved its V8 engine hard and accelerated. It was going to ram the Land Rover!

The Stig glanced in his wing mirror then yanked the handbrake, flicked the steering wheel, changed down to second and raced away hard left.

Straight up the staircase into Xenfield, a grotesque new six-storey shopping mall plonked in the heart of sleepy Bunsfold and wrong on every level.

They sped towards the atrium, their three heads banging the roof in turn as they bump-bumped up the steps. The first black van followed them while the other peeled away to the side of the building.

Terrified shoppers fled in panic.

As the Landie sped towards Xenfield's rear exit, the second sinister black van shot out of the underwear department of Marks and Spencer, crashed past the empty tables outside Starbucks and stopped dead, right in their path.

Sam thought it looked a bit less menacing covered in skinny soya latte and a pink bra and knicker set. Until the side window dropped and a bazooka popped out. Pointing straight at them.

The Stig instantly threw the ancient 4x4 into a 180-degree turn and sped back the way they'd come. Straight towards the first black Vito.

The Land Rover accelerated towards the van.

The black van accelerated towards the Land Rover.

Sam and Gramps curled into a crash position.

That's it, thought Sam. Now it's Goodnight, Vienna.

Then, with a second to spare, The Stig jammed on the handbrake, spun the Landie to the right . . . and drove straight through the open door of the glass elevator that reached to the top of the atrium.

Meanwhile, two angry black Vitos were left pointing bazookas exactly where the Land Rover wasn't any more.

As the elevator door closed behind them, The Stig reached out and hit the button for the basement. Everything was weirdly quiet, apart from the lift music – an old guitar-based instrumental called 'Jessica', by the Allman Brothers.

They'd escaped.

And in a big, sinister house up on the hill above Bunsfold there was a long, piercing scream.

TWENTY-EIGHTH

In which Sam finds it's just like riding a bike

After the crazy chase to the vet, TG's operation went almost smoothly. The Stig delivered them to the door of the animal hospital and disappeared like a toothache at the dentist's.

By 8 p.m. they were on a rather more sedate drive home, with Gramps at the wheel in full pre-war driving-test mode. At any other time Sam might have leaped out and walked in front with a red flag, but for once he was glad to be ambling.

'So that was him,' said Sam. 'Again.'

'In person,' said Gramps. 'But from what I can see he hasn't aged a bit. Which isn't possible of course . . .'

He shook his head, bewildered.

Just then, Sam picked up a text from Minnie.

> HOPE HOUND HEALTHY. ME & YR MUM
> NOW BFFS BTW. TMOZ X.

And, yes, that really was an X at the end.

It's the little things.

When they finally got back, Sam lowered the exhausted pooch gently back into her basket.

Two big brown eyes stared up at him.

'I know,' he said quietly, and stroked her head until she fell asleep.

Mum and Dad were already in bed, engrossed in screens as usual. Gramps took Sam into the living room, fetched some hot chocolate and Garibaldi biscuits and sat down next to him on the sofa. Both were quiet for a moment.

'It's no good,' said Sam bitterly. 'We've got to get away from this place, Gramps. We need to leave. All of us. Tomorrow.'

'Cut and run?' replied the veteran. 'Not really your style, is it? As my old mucker Mr Churchill pointed out after Dunkirk, "Wars are not won by evacuations."'

'You're right,' said Sam. 'This *is* a war. But it's just Minnie, Ford and me against . . . everybody. Ford Harrison is a secret genius and Minnie might be the smartest, bravest girl I've ever met, but we're only kids. And it's not just Cabriola and the Crew we're up against now. It's the whole Cruiser Corporation.'

Gramps was quiet for a moment. 'Do you remember asking me once how I survived all those missions back in the war?'

'Yup. And you said "luck",' said Sam, 'which I don't believe.'

'You're right. There *was* something else as well.'

He closed his eyes. Oh no, thought Sam. The slightly pointless just-before-I-go-to-bed nap. But he was wrong. The old man was just summoning up the past.

Gramps opened his eyes and went on. 'In the evenings, when the other pilots were playing snooker, I used to sit up in my room for hours poring over diagrams of enemy aircraft. I knew 'em inside out. Probably better than their designers.

Those planes were almost impossible to take by surprise. Machine guns and cannons on top, underneath and behind. But eventually . . . I found it.'

'What?'

'The chink,' said Gramps. 'Because, little fella, there is *always* a chink.'

Sam was listening hard. 'What was it?'

'The guns could fire in every direction . . . except one,' said Gramps quietly. And he turned and looked hard at his grandson.

'Dead ahead. You had to fly straight at them. Head on and right between the pilot's eyes. Took guts, mind. But that was the blind spot. The dead zone. The thing they least expected.' He looked at Sam intently. 'Cabriola? The Crew? The Cruiser Corporation? When you strip it all down, Sam, they're just bullies. Nothing more.' He picked up a Garibaldi and munched for a moment. 'And every bully hides a secret doubt. I think the time has come for you to fly straight at the enemy, and find out what it is.'

That was the moment – the precise instant – that Sam Wheeler knew he was ready to get back on his bike.

Gramps got up to go to bed.

'Um . . . tell Mum and Dad I'm just popping out for a walk, would you?' said Sam. 'If they even notice.'

The old man didn't look back. 'Received and understood. And don't worry – air cover's my speciality.'

Sam slipped quietly out to the garage, but when he opened

the door he stopped dead in his tracks.

Upside down on the bench was his trusty BMX. Cleaned, balanced and prepped. Turned out Gramps had been busy.

He lined up his eye with the spokes and gave the back wheel a spin. It ran true. The dent in the rim had gone and the frame looked good as new. Maybe better.

Sam turned the bike the right way up, grabbed the handlebars and weighed them in his palms. Once again he felt them twitch and come alive. But no collywobbles this time. He swung his leg over and pushed away noiselessly down the drive. It felt like coming home.

Then, in the gathering dusk, Sam 'Wheels' Wheeler finally turned north and set off, alone, for the Mansion On The Hill.

It was time for a Reckoning.

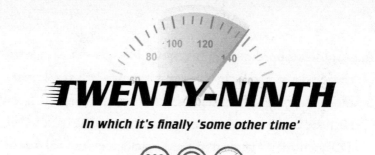

TWENTY-NINTH

In which it's finally 'some other time'

Though the sun was down it was still warm, and Sam enjoyed the breeze as he began the long climb up through the forest. It was six months since he'd last ridden, but it turned out that riding a bike is just like . . . well, riding a bike. He'd almost have enjoyed the journey if it wasn't for one thing.

He was being watched.

He shook his head to get rid of the thought, convinced he was being paranoid. But by the time the road curved east into Bunsfold Forest, the birds had stopped singing and dark clouds had gathered on the horizon.

Something was shadowing him in the trees. Something bad.

So Sam did what he always did when he was scared.

He sang. Loudly and badly. 'Yes, We Have No Bananas', followed by a horrifically tuneless version of the old 1D classic 'What Makes You Beautiful' (but certainly not with Minnie Cooper in mind. Nope. Noooo way).

And he realised, as he sang, that for now whatever-it-was was keeping a respectful distance. That or covering its ears. One or the other.

He knew he'd finally hit Cruiser Country when he spotted

a sinister black Mercedes van with blacked-out windows, skulking by the roadside. If ever a van looked as if it was helping police with their enquiries, this was it.

He rode on into the heart of the darkness.

Then, quite suddenly, two giant black gates loomed out of the half-light and towered above him, each inscribed with the Cruiser Corp's sinister logo: an unsmiling Great White Shark wearing a stylishly understated black onesie.

Sam stood in front of the gates and gazed up in wonder.

'Amazing,' he said quietly to himself. 'I didn't believe this place really existed.'

'It doesn't,' replied a low, rumbling voice over a loudspeaker.

He jumped, startled. Giant floodlights did exactly what it said on the pack: instant light flooded the area. The voice continued.

'Piranha food?' it said. 'Sling it round the back, son.'

''Scuse me?' said Sam.

'Chopped offal in the left bin, severed limbs in the right.'

'Er . . . sorry. Can't help you there. I'm here to see Cabriola. I'm a friend of hers from school.'

The loudspeaker-voice was silent for a moment. Then, 'Oh. Forget what I said about the severed limbs.'

A familiar female voice grabbed the microphone.

'Spooner? Hummer? What on earth are you doing up here at this time of night? Chainsaw Practice is tomorrow. Go away.'

'It's not Spummer,' said Sam. 'It's the new kid.'

Silence. He went on.

'You know. Hippy-haired speccy scaredy-cat? Ring any bells?'

Another pause, then the girl's voice returned. 'Well, well. Ditched the stabilisers, I see. And what can I do for you?'

'Well, you see, Cabriola, I'm peckish. So I've popped out for a snack.'

'And what's that got to do with me, exactly?'

'Well, what I *really* fancied was some . . . cheesy Wotsits.'

The girl took a moment to reply.

'The way I and thirty other kids remember it, new kid, you chickened out of the challenge when you had the chance.'

'Nope. I said "some other time",' replied Sam. 'And this is some other time.'

'I see,' drawled Cabriola. 'All right. Challenge accepted. I'll see you in the playground at 8 a.m. This should be fun.'

'Not this time, Miss Cruiser. No crowds. No quips. No grandstanding. Just you and me. Here. Tonight.'

'Sorry, new kid. Daddy doesn't like me talking to boys outside after bedtime. He's old-fashioned that way.'

'I'm not sure Daddy cares much *what* you do,' said Sam.

There was an indignant scream from the loudspeaker.

And there it is, right there, thought Sam in a burst of blinding clarity.

The chink.

Cabriola returned, her composure recovered. 'All right, new kid. Let's do this.'

'Don't forget the Wotsits.'

'Oh, I wouldn't worry about those,' she said. 'The only

thing you'll be eating tonight is mud.'

A moment later the giant gates slid apart and the sleek BMX-from-the-next-century hurtled out, twist-jumped in mid-air and skidded to a halt millimetres from his front toe.

Cabriola stared at him hard. 'The giant oak tree by the rec. Know it?'

Sam nodded.

'First to touch it wins,' she said. 'There are no other rules.'

'One rule,' said Sam. 'Whatever happens tonight stays between us. This is about you and me. Deal?'

'Well, I can see why you'd want it that way. Okay, new kid. Deal.'

And she was gone.

Sam whipped after her, taking up station a few lengths behind to shadow any move she'd pull.

At least, that was the idea. Unfortunately, ten seconds later the future-BMX in front of him was pulling away like a train.

Blimey. This girl could ride. *Really* ride.

And then the rain came. The dark clouds that had been gathering all evening ripped open and every trail turned to mud. Sam could hardly see for water on his specs.

Up ahead, Cabriola's dim outline was dancing between the trees in the moonlight and pulling relentlessly away.

This wasn't going to plan. If she got out of sight, it was game over. And he was tiring.

He needed to snap his head into gear, and fast. Focus, Wheeler!

So he summoned up visions of anything that would drive him harder.

His wounded dog. Charade's contorted sneer. Minnie's understanding smile. The tricycle. Ford's heroic one-man stand in BCHQ. Gramps.

And suddenly he wasn't tired any more.

He pulled left out of a mud-trail and found a clear run.

Now the bike was coming alive. It felt like part of him again. The gap was closing. He flew between the tree roots, boy and bike as one.

The oak tree was in sight. There were just eighty metres to go and it was the final charge for the line.

He feinted left, feinted left again then ducked right and pulled alongside. And, as he did so, Cabriola Cruiser – undefeated in eight Wotsits Challenges – turned, startled, to find him right beside her.

And he could see in her eyes that she was beaten.

He was past. First by a length. Then three. Then five. It was game over.

Only it turned out it wasn't.

Because ten metres short of the giant oak tree, and well in the lead, Sam Wheeler suddenly stopped dead in his tracks.

Cabriola slowed as she approached him, looking confused and exhausted. She cycled carefully past, braked to a halt, reached out and touched the tree.

She'd won.

The two kids stood silently staring at each other in the rain.

Finally, Sam spoke. 'Congratulations.' He pulled a sodden packet of cheesy Wotsits from his pocket and handed it to her. 'Now tell me, what did we prove?'

Still she said nothing.

'You know, there's one thing I just don't get,' said Sam. He took off his glasses and dried them. 'Why do you act like a bully?'

The girl gazed into the distance. Then she wiped the rain from her face, turned away and said simply, 'It's complicated.'

Without another word, Sam Wheeler turned to ride away.

And Cabriola Cruiser watched after him in silence until he disappeared.

THIRTIETH

In which Sam finally calls the cops

Every day started pretty much the same at Bunsfold High, and Fridays were no different. Arrive, hang around in playground, get hassled by an idiot bully. Standard.

So when Sam, Minnie and Ford arrived to find the gate blocked by Dennis Charade and his bike, it wasn't exactly a surprise.

'So . . . is it *some other time yet,* new kid?' asked the weasely one, with a stupid grin.

Sam took off his specs and wiped them on his school shirt. He was still tired after the Wotsits Showdown. He wasn't late. He could wait.

Behind him he heard the all-too-familiar sound of Narnium brakes on space-age wheels as Cabriola Cuiser pulled up.

'Budge,' she said to Charade.

He moved back just far enough to let her through but still block the other three.

'All the way.'

Charade held up his hand for a high-five. Cabriola ignored it entirely, with the expression of someone who has just detected a fart.

Charade tried again. 'Seems Three-Wheeler has forgotten his tricycle, boss!'

Silence.

'HA HA!' he laughed nervously.

'Charade . . .' said Cabriola flatly, looking at her wannabe henchman with distaste. 'Go away.'

As she passed by, she turned and nodded almost imperceptibly at Sam. If you weren't looking for it, you'd have missed it. Sam was looking for it.

Then she pushed her once-unbeatable bike on towards the classroom, followed at a respectful distance by a crestfallen Charade.

'Love the new school bag, boss!' he gabbled.

Again, silence. And now Charade was starting to look properly jumpy.

'I saw HIM AGAIN LAST NIGHT . . .' he blurted after her. 'IN THE WOODS.'

Cabriola stopped and, without turning, tilted her head fractionally to one side.

'You saw . . . who?'

'You know . . . *him*. The weird geezer in the white racing suit.'

Cabriola, Sam, Minnie and Ford all turned to him as one.

'Where?' said Minnie.

'When?' said Cabriola.

'Oh, on my way home.'

Cabriola looked sceptical. Charade went on.

'Yeah. Said he's here for the race. On Saturday. I told him to forget it. That no one's as quick as you around that course.'

'So he actually spoke,' said Cabriola. 'To you.'

Dennis Charade blinked and took a breath. He wasn't entirely sure of his ground, but he had an audience. This was where he came alive.

'Definitely.' The kids looked at him expectantly. 'He said he could when he really needed to, and would I not tell anyb– Oh. Well, it's out now.'

Then the bell went.

Sam turned to Ford as they filed into the hall. 'Tell me, why does Charade lie all the time?' he asked.

Ford shrugged. 'No idea,' he replied. 'Why does a goat jump?'

After another screen-filled break time, Sam made a decision.

This had all gone on too long.

A disappeared headmaster, a disappeared boy, a dog being attacked and an entire town addicted to a computer game. And severed limbs fed to piranhas. Severed from *what*, exactly? It was time to blow the whistle.

'I'm going to the cops,' he said to Ford and Minnie. 'Straight after school. Coming?'

'Hang on,' said Ford. 'We're piecing it together ourselves. And . . .'

'And we're just three pesky kids. We're out of our depth. So let's dump this on someone else's desk.'

'All right.' Minnie shrugged. 'It could hardly make things worse.'

So after school the three friends wandered into town, resisted the lure of the sweet shop – nearly – and ascended the unworn steps of the sleepy police station.

They found themselves in a waiting area with two chairs, a sliding glass window and a noticeboard announcing that the streets were to be closed the following weekend for a huge international go-kart race, all costs picked up by the Cruiser Corporation.

The window opened.

'Evening, all,' said a cheery man's voice. 'What can I do for you?'

'Um . . .' said Sam. 'Hard to know where to start, but basically we think the whole town – and possibly the world – is in danger.'

'The whole wide world, eh?' said the officer. 'That *does* sound big. Why don't we start at the beginning? You tell me everything, I'll take notes, and we'll see where we go from there. How does that sound?'

Sam thought it sounded like a polite brush-off, but after turning to Ford and Minnie – one shrug, one nod – he began.

About three pages in, the duty officer held up his hand for a pause, and called over his shoulder to someone inside the station, 'Inspector Hallam, some back-up, please.'

Soon he was joined at the window by a smart woman in plain clothes.

'Sergeant?'

'Deafbot. One T or two?'

'I'd say one,' said the inspector. 'If it's named after what it sounds like, a robot that can't hear – is that what it is? Kids?'

'Two,' said Ford. 'One in Death, one in bot.'

'Oh, DEATHbot,' said the sergeant and the inspector together.

'I'm glad you've cleared that up, young man,' said the sergeant. 'Imagine how silly we'd have looked, making a report about an earless android when all the time it's a homicidal cyborg. We'd never have lived it down.'

Sam was fuming. The officers were clearly having fun at their expense.

'We're not making this up!' said Ford before Sam could.

'You have to admit that it all sounds a bit far-fetched,' said the inspector. She was skimming through the sergeant's report as she spoke. 'Global mind control via a computer game? Killer robots in the woods? Stolen dogs? Severed limbs fed to petunias?'

'Piranhas,' said the sergeant. 'Honestly, my handwriting.'

The inspector sighed. 'Listen. Everybody knows there's been trouble in Bunsfold recently. We haven't found many clues so far about the missing Mustang boy or your headmaster. And this Xenon game does sound unhealthily amazi— I mean, addictive. So why don't you come inside and finish the story? We might even throw in a cuppa and a biccy if you're lucky. Deal?'

It sounded better than staying crowded in the corridor speaking through a hatch to a patronising sergeant, so in they trooped.

When they'd finished, Inspector Hallam agreed to send a squad car up to MOTH and have a quiet word with the town's only dillionaire. Never mind the fact that since his arrival the annual Policeman's Ball had been held monthly, in Mauritius, by private jet, or that the current squad-car fleet contained three blue-and-white Ferrari 488 panda cars and a Bugatti Chiron with a light on top. PT Cruiser was a citizen like anyone else, and if investigations were required he was most certainly NOT above the law. Oh no.

The kids left feeling slightly more reassured. If there really were killer fish and evil robots up there, the cops would flush it out. It was a relief to have some grown-up help on their side at last.

Sam snuck a look into the car park as they left. Bugattis? Ferraris? Something wasn't adding up.

'Celebratory Cornetto?' offered Ford.

'Sure,' said Sam. 'Keep mine cool. I'm just going back to check on something.'

He ran back up the steps and into the waiting area. He heard voices through the hatch. He kept his head down.

'So are we actually going to visit MOTH, ma'am?'

'Certainly, Sergeant. But with the shocking level of litter in the duck pond – not to mention security for the church bingo night and the world's press arriving next week for the race –

I'm rather busy right now, aren't you?'

'Absolutely, ma'am. Snowed under. And, ma'am, I have a question, if I may?'

'Go on, Sergeant.'

'Ahem . . . what's your high score?'

Sam risked a peek over the window ledge to see both police officers reach silently for their Xenon consoles.

THIRTY-FIRST

The Boy who cried Wolf

Dennis Charade liked to boast that he was pretty fearless. He'd even persuaded himself. So the shortcut through the woods was still his preferred route home. Even at dusk.

Stay out of the woods? he thought. Not Dennis Charade. I'd like to see some creepy creature try to catch *me*. Fat chance!

But an uneasy feeling crept in. This was handover time, when the hares and rabbits scamper home to leave the forest to the creatures of the night. The owls, the foxes, the bats and . . . well, who knows what.

He was almost sure he heard a rustling over to the left. Probably just a bird stuck in a thicket. He shook his head to clear it and rode quickly towards the narrow bridge where he'd boasted about seeing the White Weirdo.

Wouldn't it be crazy, he thought, if I actually did?

Just then, with some relief, he made out the lanky figure of Simon Spooner, sitting on a branch over the bridge. What was he doing out here?

Result! He never got to hang out after school with the Crew, and the rest of the gang wouldn't be far away. Cabriola would see good ol' Dennis, the Bunsfold Cowboy, riding through the woods as the light faded like the plucky kid in a film. Like the kid he totally was. As they'd now see.

The idea made him feel almost sick with anticipation. Or maybe it was all the bouncing over the tree roots.

Calm, Dennis, he told himself. Play it cool.

'Yo, Spooner, my man,' he said. ''Sup?'

'Fancy seeing you here,' said the long-limbed lad on the branch. 'Seen your mate The Stig yet?'

'Stigster? Sure!' said Dennis out of habit. 'Just back there.'

'Yeah? Show me.'

'Sure!' said Dennis, without thinking. 'So where's the Crew?'

'Busy,' said Spooner. 'So show me.'

'Oh, he won't be there now. He moves fast, see. And he doesn't reveal himself to just anyone. You have to gain his trust, get his respect. No offence, but –'

'None taken. I'd still like to see. Get as close to the legend as I can.'

Charade looked at Spooner, considered, and then said something he'd liked the sound of when he heard Sam Wheeler say it.

'Some other time.'

Spooner jumped down from the branch. He landed in a surprisingly graceful manner – less baby giraffe, more well-oiled machine – and came right up to Charade. He leaned over in a way that if Dennis hadn't known him better would have seemed a tiny bit menacing.

'No,' said Spooner. 'Show me now.'

Remembering how the new Wheeler kid had handled this same bully back in the playground, Charade suddenly thought of a way to take the boorish beanpole down a peg or two.

'I have to say, Spooner,' he said, 'that you have very mad banners. What do you have?'

'I don't have any banners, you little fool. Let alone mad ones. Now stop wasting my time and show me where you saw . . . *him.*'

'Soz,' said Dennis. 'Gotta get back for supper. Hey, let go of my – Ow!'

Spooner was holding tighter now. 'That way?' he hissed. 'Or THAT way?'

'Get off! I warn you I'm a black belt in . . . *Grrmmmph!*'

Now Spooner had his hand over his mouth, and Dennis could hardly breathe.

And just then he realised that he wasn't talking to Simon Spooner at all.

He looked up at the thing looming above him and shuddered. It was beginning to look less and less human. The narrow eyes started to change shape – then melt like a waxwork placed too close to the fire. The pale flesh peeled away and morphed into a harder, shinier, much darker surface. Where the eyes had been, red lights appeared: dim at first, but coming into focus as they spelled out a series of words that Dennis Charade hardly recognised.

The truth.

NAME . . . DENNIS GERVAISE CHARADE . . . DATE

OF BIRTH . . . 14 MAY . . . SCHOOL . . . BUNSFOLD HIGH . . . BLOOD GROUP . . . A RHESUS POSITIVE . . .

The figure reached out a metallic finger and shot something into the boy's neck.

DISLIKES: OWNING UP . . . WETTING BED . . . GREEN VEG . . . VEG IN GENERAL . . . LIKES . . . TELLING PORKIES . . . CABRIOLA CRUISER . . .

The world was slipping away, but still the data streamed on. Then a high-pitched beep, and the result it had been looking for:

DEEPEST FEAR: THE BAD TEDDY BEAR IN *TOY STORY 3*.

The visor cleared for a moment before slowly turning into a cuddly pink teddy face with a big blackcurrant nose . . . Then it stopped.

OH, THIS IS RIDICULOUS.

Another high-pitched beep, then:

SECOND DEEPEST FEAR: BEING HYPNOTISED

The dark shape developed spiral circles where the eyes would have been. They began to spin, slowly at first and then faster and faster. Dennis was terrified. He'd seen someone hypnotised in a theatre once, and they'd blurted out all sorts of things – all of them true.

What if that happened to him? They might find out that he . . . or that he'd never . . . It was too scary to think about. He could feel his eyes drooping. He was sinking into a trance. Must . . . stay . . . awake . . .

The dark helmet leaned in even closer and, through his stupor, Dennis caught a new message on the visor:

WHERE . . . IS . . . THE STIG?

I don't know! thought Dennis as he slipped away in panic. Why . . . ? What are you going to do with him?

GRIND HIS BONES TO MAKE MY BREAD.

Now Charade was terrified. 'I'll tell you anything. I still sleep with an undersheet . . . I haven't moved on to grown-up toothpaste . . .'

The figure shuddered with almost human impatience as it waited for a gap in this stream of irrelevance. Finally it wound the spinning eyes up to maximum and flashed a message in extra-bright LEDs:

WHERE . . . IS . . . THE STIG?

The boy came to his senses. In a panic, he blurted it all out.

'I made it up! I make everything up. I'd tell you everything, but I don't know anything. I was just . . . boasting! I'm not all bad! Honest! I get the shopping for my mum! I'm all right on a bike! I'm quite good at science!'

SCIENCE?

I MET SOME SCIENTISTS ONCE.

THEY TASTE LIKE CHICKEN.

'What?' screamed Dennis. 'You . . . you . . . *ate* them?'

JUST THE LIVER . . . WITH SOME BAKED BEANS AND A NICE KIWI SMOOTHIE . . . SLURP-SLURP-SLURP.

'Noooo! Please don't hurt me! I don't know anything! I just make things up to impress people. And . . .'

The figure couldn't have been less impressed. As Dennis finally collapsed on the bumpy forest floor, it flashed a last red message.

GOING DOWN.

THIRTY-SECOND

In which TG Dog steps up

The plucky mongrel opens one eye to make sure.

Her nose is working fine: she's back in the garage, just as she thought. Back where the kind old Gramps man had helped her to get better, until she leaped up to save the hairy boy Sam from the Very Bad Thing.

She'd been recovering, then ripped her leg again, but that's instinct for you. What could she do? She's a dog.

And then the mad race in the bumpy car up to the white-coat place, with all its rooms that smelled of too much clean, but which were welcome after all the odd smells coming from the strange white helmet man. What had *he* been eating?

With humans she can normally tell: this one loves custard, this one oranges, this one may as well be a dog himself for all the veg he eats. But the fast one in the white suit who wouldn't bark? He had her stumped. Where were the clues in smelling like an unstuck plaster or an orphaned badger cub?

But one thing was for sure: he'd got her there, and disappeared only when he saw she was safe.

She tries to stand. She has to start moving. It's been too long. Her best friend, Buster, is still in the cage. He needs her, and she needs him too. She has to get him back. She stands: three paws on the cold floor. Now for the tricky one: the left hind leg.

It hurts, but works. She walks. The floor is cold.

Limp to the door. Push with the nose. Not locked.

She sniffs: coast clear. Walk out. The grass is wet, but warmer than the garage floor. The moon is up. She breaks into a run. She pants. She checks. She's fine. She carries on.

Each night for nine moons she would run up to the Bad House where her best friend is trapped. But all this week she couldn't run: couldn't catch her breath. But now she has to try.

Get Buster!

She picks up pace. Her leg feels fine. She stays out of the light. She takes the road that leads to the woods. She finds the place where she last saw her friend: the bridge, where that tall creature – that Bad Thing – held her friend Buster by the . . . She gives a thick, low growl. She snarls. One day. One day.

And every dog has its day.

A flash of movement to the left.

A vixen! How very *dare* she! These are MY woods. Oi! Brush-baby! If I catch you around here again, I'll . . .

Not now. Discipline, TG. There will be other nights, different dumb foxes who need a lesson in who's boss.

She knows now how not to be caught. Up, up she pads, past trees she knows by night and day; they hide her, warn her, stand tall. On her side. Until she wees on them. No, honestly, they're fine with it. Some of her best friends are trees.

Which reminds her. The bins, and the small red eye that lives in them. She times her run, leaps up – ow, mind the leg – and leaves a little present right on top. Now the eye can't see until the wind blows hard, or someone comes to clean. Serves them right. She runs on until she finds the pipe. The pipe that goes up to the Bad House. She found it first six moons back. Stank then. Stinks now. She likes most things that smell, but not this. And it's so long, so wet, so smooth. No grip. She slips. Her leg hurts. She goes on. Up and up. It's a long pipe. It smells of poop. It's where poop goes to die.

She tries to hold her breath, but has to pant. She scrambles up until at last she sees the light.

Aaaand breathe.

The things she does for Buster.

Another light now. Not the moon. This shines from the huge lamps that make the night so bright around the Bad House. Sweeping round, leaving it dark where they've just been. She's learned to time her run. So she waits, and runs at the right time, up to the fence and the hole she dug all those weeks past. She moves the twigs she's laid there, crawls through and pricks her ears. She hears a sound.

Thump, bounce, thud.

A sound she knows of old! Can it be . . . ?

It has to be. He did the same thing back at home against the garage door, way back when she remembers living there. For an hour or more: the ball, the throw, the catch, the ball . . . She would watch with love, and at times would fetch the ball when he got bored and threw it for her to fetch.

Thump, bounce, thud. It must be him, and this must be the night. The night she finds him. Finally!

She thought she heard it some moons past but could not get the scent: too far away. But now she can feel him. She looks up at the lights. Down to the ground. A red beam. She can sense it, at the same height as her head.

Not this time, sunshine.

She drops flat, drags herself under the beam.

Made it.

She finds the wall. She sniffs. She gets the scent. It's him! A wall away, that's all. She doesn't risk a bark. A scratch: a tiny whine.

The noise stops. *Thump, bounce* . . . then still. A pause. A voice. A voice she knows.

'TG? Is that you? Scratch if –'

Scratch.

'TG! You made it! How you doin'? Come here! Let me feel you. Let me . . .'

Boy and dog each nudge close to their side of the wall, moving as if they touch for real, boy to dog and dog to boy, as if there is no wall in between.

'It's not safe, girl,' he whispers. 'You have to go. They'll find you. How did you find me? Sometimes I swear I've heard you, but it's never you. Unless . . . Have you been here before? TG? Have you . . . ?'

She hears the voice she loves. The words are sounds, and

sounds she knows are meant for her, but just sounds all the same. But then a sound she knows:

'Get Ford,' he says. 'Get Fordo! Where's Fordo? Fetch Ford. TG! Fetch Fordo!'

She gives a different scratch. Rubs her head up to the wall as if to say, yes, I know Ford. I know Fordo.

I'll fetch him.

Hold on.

I'll fetch Fordo for you.

THIRTY-THIRD

In which Cabriola Cruiser meets someone she's never met before

It was race week, and the whole town was abuzz.

But Dennis Charade wasn't around to make the most of it, boasting how his dad had secured the best VIP seats next to Posh, Becks and the Trumps. Instead he was nowhere to be seen.

On the Friday before race day, exactly a week after he'd last been in school, he was back. But it was hardly the same old Dennis that shuffled into class that morning. Instead of boasting, he was staring into the middle distance, gibbering quietly to himself.

'Don't . . . don't eat me! Not *me* . . .' Then, 'He's out there! In the forest! I saw him! Bad. Very bad. Very tall. Very bad. I SAW THE DEATHBOT!'

Cabriola Cruiser was the first to lose it. 'Charade, you muppet, shut UP!'

Even Minnie Cooper slammed down her books in frustration.

'Oh, for HEAVEN'S SAKE, Charade. What do you take us for? You, The Stig and the Deathbot all chilling in the forest? For once – just once – could you stop LYING!'

Charade looked up her with bloodshot eyes.

'He'll grind your bones to make his bread.' Then he turned to stare, wild-eyed, at Spooner, before raising a quivering arm and slowly pointing at him.

'You!' Then a gulp. 'It pre– it pretended to be . . . you!'

'Aww, don't worry, Den,' said the henchman, looking nonplussed. 'Probably just a milly six-up.'

The classroom door slammed shut and Rodius marched in – smelling, as usual, as if a small woodland mammal had crawled up his bottom and died.

Then, just as the lesson was getting into its normal nightmarish swing of hurtling chalk and whack-a-mole, they were interrupted.

They heard them before they saw them. The distant throb of approaching V8 supercar motors.

Three sinister-looking black vans burst straight through the school gates, swerved across the playground and screeched to a halt right outside the classroom block.

Men in black suits and dark glasses jumped out, looked left and right and whispered into their sleeves.

Last to emerge – and clearly in charge – was Maurice Marina, who calmly strode into the building, clomped down the corridor and burst through the classroom door.

Rodius turned to him furiously. 'WHAT is the meaning of this INTERRUP—'

'Shut up,' said Maurice without looking at him. And Rodius did. Instantly.

'Er . . . 'scuse me, Miss Cabriola, but your dad wants to see you. Now.'

All heads swung to the back row.

Cabriola Cruiser dropped her anti-Rodius breathing mask. 'He . . . wants . . . to *see* me?'

'Yes. And that's exactly what I just said.'

'But . . . he's never . . .' She'd gone very pale. Then she caught the expectant expressions of her watching classmates, and got back into character.

'Certainly, Maurice. Fetch my things and follow me,' she said smoothly, unfurling herself from her desk like a snow leopard.

So it was that just a few moments later Maurice Marina led Cabriola Cruiser for the very first time down the long and mysterious hallway towards the mysterious lair of her mysterious father.

If she was nervous, it didn't show, though someone watching closely might have caught the smallest suggestion of a trembling upper lip. It's not every day a girl gets to meet her dillionaire father for the first time, after all.

Eventually they reached the endlessly tall Narnium doors at the end of the corridor. At her approach, they slid noiselessly upwards.

A short, beardy man wearing nothing but a stylishly understated black onesie was standing in the middle of a large, dark room facing her, his hands behind his back.

He looked uncomfortable.

She looked uncomfortable.

Nobody said anything.

Eventually, PT Cruiser stepped towards her. 'Hey! Fist bump!' he said, with forced jauntiness. But then he high-fived her instead, his open palm missing her fist by some distance.

Silence.

'Awkward!' said PT.

Cabriola said nothing.

'Well!' said PT eventually. 'I'm so glad we've had this talk.' And he turned to walk away. 'Goodbye!'

Maurice cleared his throat. 'Ahem . . . 'scuse me, boss. The plan?'

'Ah yes,' said PT. 'Cabriola, I haven't been the most attentive of fathers. In fact, I've never met you before.'

Cabriola said nothing. He went on.

'But I've always been there for you. In my own way. You know. Watching.'

Silence.

'Anyway. I wanted to tell you in person that the time has come to finally . . . bring you into the family business.'

Whereupon Cabriola's eyes widened momentarily. Now *this* was a turn-up. 'You have my attention,' she said matter-of-factly.

'Yes, Project Daught– I mean, Cabriola. The moment you win the event tomorrow – and Xenon is launched upon the entire human race – you will become the new CEO – that's like *boss* – of the entire Cruiser Corporation! Have you any idea what this means? You will be, officially and indisputably, the Richest Brat In The World!'

Cabriola flushed. Her eyes brightened.

PT went on. 'You will have to leave school immediately, of course. You will have a billion-dollar salary. And houses and polo ponies all over the world. And rock stars, royalty and politicians queuing up to kiss your butt.'

Cabriola inadvertently half-smiled.

PT went on. 'You will have a holiday entitlement of fifty-one weeks and six days a year. You will have a Ferrari LaFerrari as your Company Car. And you will have Liam from One Direction.'

'Er . . . what?'

'Yes, I've bought him for you. You like him very much, I think? I checked your internet search history.'

Cabriola was quiet for a moment.

'All right,' she said quietly, her eyes shining softly. 'I'm in.'

'Yay!' said PT. 'You go, girl!'

And he went to hug her just as she went to fist-bump him, so her fist went straight into his tummy. They parted awkwardly.

'One question. Why now?'

'Weeeell . . .' he wheezed, still winded, 'I guess there comes a time in every dillionaire's life when his thoughts turn to . . . you know . . . *legacy*. And because I'd like to make amends for my lifelong lack of interest in you. And because there are tax advantages.' He paused. 'Actually, it's mainly the tax advantages.'

'I see,' said Cabriola. 'All this as soon as the race finishes?'

'Correct. The moment you win, I hand over the reins. The keys to the kingdom. While I retire to oversee my charity, the Cruiser Foundation, donating dillions to good causes. Lifeboats. Donkeys. That kind of thing.' He smiled, rubbing his hands. 'Yes . . . just as you take the chequered flag . . . and a humiliated, last-placed Stig is destroyed forever . . .'

'Er . . . what?' said Cabriola.

PT had that Did-I-just-say-that-out-loud? expression again. He looked at Maurice, who coughed uneasily.

'It's a trap, isn't it?' said Cabriola. 'The race, I mean. It's all just a trap . . . to catch – *him*.'

'Maybe,' said PT rather quietly.

'But *why*?' asked Cabriola.

The dillionaire took a deep breath. 'You know when a fly buzzes around your kitchen,' he said, 'and you grab a tea towel, but just can't get it? It lands; you swing. You swing; it lands. You miss; it buzzes around your head, winking a hundred and twelve eyes at you. But then – just occasionally – gotcha!'

'Sort of.'

'Well, The Stig is my fly. And you're my tea towel.'

'Oh, well, that's a relief,' said Cabriola. 'And there was me thinking you had a hopeless man-crush on him.'

'WHO THE HELL IS GOING AROUND TELLING EVERYONE THAT?' said PT.

Maurice coughed again. The dillionaire composed himself. 'Daughter. All this is about to be yours, but be aware that

Forces are gathering against us.' And he paused, and looked solemn. 'The Forces of Lightness.'

'Don't worry,' said Cabriola. 'I can beat him, you know.'

'Oh, I know. You were bred for it. Your DNA is a custom-designed genetic porridge containing strands from every great racing driver in history. You have been trained, evolved and perfected for this since birth. Your Kart is unbeatable. Also, we're going to nobble him.'

'NO! I can do it on my own. Without your help.'

'What . . . like you beat the Wheeler boy to the tree the other night?'

Cabriola was silent for a moment. Then: 'I see. So you've been watching me.'

'Well, duh,' said PT. 'Though technically I was watching Mr Wheeler. Or my colleague the Deathbot was observing him for me. The Deathbot has been watching him for a while, you see. Rather closer than he realises.'

Cabriola was silent. There was much to take in. And most of it was good. Really good.

Then, finally . . .

'How do you know he'll turn up? I mean, it's so obviously a trap.'

PT threw his head back, and laughed. 'HA! Oh, he'll turn up. He can't help himself. That's what's so marvellous about Mr The Stig. You see, for him, racing is all there is.'

And he paused for a moment.

'Everything else is just . . . waiting.'

THIRTY-FOURTH

In which we glimpse the power of Xenon

Ford Harrison treated himself to a well-deserved box of Jammie Dodgers. And then another.

Operation Woo Minnie Cooper couldn't fail.

The moment he'd heard about Excavation 3000, the archaeology conference about historically significant shallow trenches, he knew he had to get two tickets. Now he just had to engineer things so Minnie was always in the trench and he on the edge, and bingo. Equal terms. He was convinced they'd see eye to eye on this one.

What with Project High Hair finally lasting a full three hours between charges and the Rocket as ready as it would ever be, things were definitely looking up. Unlike him, once it all went to plan.

He steeled himself for the evening's second task: the Xenon Experiment.

It was the day before the planned global launch, and the time had finally come to play it. Could it possibly be as don't-look-back awesome as everyone said?

What if he became addicted, like everyone else?

But if he wanted to understand the enemy, he saw no way

round it. And, sure, he was fascinated. If what he'd heard was true, the game meant something different to everyone. Like a horoscope, you saw what you needed to see. It spoke to you alone. The imaginary friend who knew you better than you knew yourself. The father that you never . . . leave it there, Ford. Focus.

They'd read *The Odyssey* at school last year. About this bloke trying to get home from Troy and meeting all sorts of dangers on the way. The Sirens sounded the worst: wicked spirits with voices so beautiful that sailors couldn't help sailing towards them, only to get shipwrecked on the rocks.

Odysseus had tied himself to the mast so he couldn't steer his ship towards the Sirens. Ford needed his version of that.

So he'd spent days perfecting it. First, get a console. No problem there: they were literally giving them away.

Then attach himself to his chair, leaving his hands free to play.

Then place his console on the ejector seat, and programme it to detonate after precisely five minutes. So the thing would be shooting out through the hole in the roof and surprising a squirrel by the time Sam turned up.

Now for the moment of truth.

Handcuffs: check. Click, cli– Hang on. Think. No, all covered. It was time.

He threw the key across the floor – visible to anyone coming in, but impossible to reach from the chair. He was ready.

He pressed *Activate Xenon Initiation.*

Oh no. The loo. He knew there was something. Damn.

BZZZZZZZZeeeeeooooowwwww eeehhhhhoooooooooo . . .

That sound! From the backs of buses, the hands of roadworkers, lollipop men and women . . . it used to drive him bonkers with annoyance. SHUT the beep UP! Now it wasn't annoying at all. Rather lovely, in fact. Like singing a lullaby. With a toasted sandwich. In a Bristol Motors garage. At Christmas. To Minnie. In a trench. All perfect. For him.

He began to play. And suddenly the idea of a precautionary wee felt as distant as Neptune.

Whump! Sam Wheeler landed with the customary thump on the floor of the Den.

'Hello?' he said, seeing Ford on the chair.

No answer.

'So I'm five minutes late. No need for the silent treatment. I've got a great idea to help us find the . . . Ford? Are you okay?'

'More than okay,' said Ford in a strange voice. 'I've seen the future, and it's . . . wonderful. I think. As far as I –'

'Wouldn't be anything to do with this, would it?' said Sam, holding up a smashed console. 'I found it by the path, next to an unusually angry squirrel. You haven't been . . . ? What's this key doing here?'

'Cuffs. Can't be too careful. And, yes, I've been behind enemy lines. Here, unlock me and hand over that console, will you? See if I can't get it to work again.'

'Fat chance,' said Sam, shoving the broken console in his bag before freeing his friend. 'So?'

BZZZZZZZZeeeeeoooowwwww eeehhhhhoooooooooo . . .

Ford didn't seem to hear. He was humming the Xenon initiation fanfare to himself and rocking gently back and forth.

Sam tried to find his friend behind the staring eyes.

'What's it like, then?' he asked.

'Beyond all imagining. It's . . .'

'Don't tell me. *Everything.* But what sort of everything? How does it work? Where do you start? How does it hook you so fast?'

'Well, it . . . You . . .' Ford stopped. After a range of increasingly pained expressions, his shoulders slumped.

'I can't remember,' he said. 'Not a thing about it.' And he paused for a moment, and looked up at Sam. 'Except that it was marvellous.'

Sam recalled the kid at the rec saying the same.

He turned round to catch Ford rummaging desperately in his bag for the console.

'Ford!' he shouted. 'Get a grip!'

Ford sat down again, stunned. What had this thing done to him? Sam threw the console to the floor and jumped on it. No use: it still gave a faint beep and a weak, winking red light. He took it over to the sink, prised it open with a kitchen knife, smeared peanut butter all over the working parts then dumped it in a bowl of greasy washing-up water.

Finally Ford spoke, more like himself.

'We have to stop the launch. We can't let it happen. It's too . . . *everything*.'

'I gathered,' said Sam. 'So we need to get into MOTH.'

'Can't be done,' said Ford, shaking his head as if coming out of a swimming pool – or a nightmare. 'I've studied the plans. They weren't that hard to find online, but getting inside will be impossible. There's no way in.'

'Cabriola gets in and out every day.'

'No way in *for us,* I mean. Cameras all over. They have this whole town covered. Then lasers – break one beam and you not only trip all the alarms, you also lose whatever body part you touched it with. And assuming you can figure out a way of getting through, there are the armed drones. Shoot first; ask questions later. Actually, strike that. Shoot first, shoot later.'

'Okay, that sounds serious,' agreed Sam. 'But –'

'And, in case anything goes wrong with them, there's a colony of actual live ninjas. With the curvy swords and the black masks and everything.'

'Okay, so we –'

'And if by some miracle you get through them and the toxic acid moat, there's the bear pit. It automatically sprays anyone that falls in with spawning-salmon-in-honey-glaze scent. Which would drive the grizzlies berserk, I imagine.'

'Blimey, they really don't like visitors, do they?'

Ford sighed. 'Nope. It is, to all intents, impregnable.'

Sam was quiet for a moment. Then he shook his head. 'Trust me,' he said. 'There is *always* a chink.'

THIRTY-FIFTH

In which TG Dog takes the lead

Ford admired his new friend's optimism. He wasn't short of it himself. It was just that he liked to think around problems rather than straight through them. Like Odysseus.

'Finding a chink, Samuel,' he said, 'may not be possible. It seems PT Cruiser has watched every *Mission: Impossible* film and copied all the impossible bits.'

Sam thought about it. The bears, the beams, the ninjas . . .

'Okay. So what's our Plan B?'

'Plan B –' Ford shrugged – 'is less direct, but smarter. We win the race.'

He walked over to the Bunsfold Rocket and patted the rear spoiler.

'She's almost set. Our Trojan horse.'

'Trojan donkey, more like. If their bikes are anything to go by, then Team Cruiser's go-karts will be streets ahead. Whole towns.'

'Yes, I've calculated that whatever beast they put up will be packing at least three times the power, and Narnium efficiency. Anything I can knock up in here will look like an also-ran at best. But . . .'

'But?'

'Remember when I thought someone was secretly tweaking it?'

Sam nodded. 'The elves?'

'They still are,' said Ford. 'Only now they're ripping bits off. At first I thought the kart was being nobbled; now I see it's not that at all. The elves are adding . . . lightness.' He took a deep breath. 'And I think I know who the elf is.'

'You think it's *him*,' said Sam. 'The Stig. That he's planning to race and save the world.'

'I'm counting on it.'

'Well, I guess it's our only shot,' sighed Sam. 'I've seen him drive and, trust me, there's nothing he can't do on four wheels. But what if he doesn't turn up? It's such an obvious trap. I vote we continue on both fronts. Mind if I look at the plans myself? With Minnie, maybe. She doesn't give up easily. Which reminds me. Must bounce. Off out with her tonight.'

Ford turned to him and stared. He'd gone a little pale. 'Oh . . . I see, well, of course you must go. Don't want to be late. Hot date, eh?'

Sam shifted a little.

'No, I, um, just said I'd call when I was free, maybe hook up for an iced tea tonight in town. I mean, you're busy, right? With the kart and the plans and stuff?'

'Right,' said Ford. 'See you.'

'See y– OOah!'

Sam went flying over something on the floor. He stood,

holding up a pair of trainers with what looked like some sort of hydraulic elevating platform on the underside.

'These yours?'

Ford took them silently and turned away towards the kart.

'Work to do,' he said quietly. 'Have fun.'

Sam slipped out by the side door and Ford sat for a while, dealing with thoughts.

Before long, the air was split by a chorus of car horns playing La Cucaracha, just out of sync with each other.

Dee diddle EEE-dee, de diddle EEE-dee, deedle deedle deedle dee.

What's he forgotten now? thought Ford, checking the intruder alarm. No, the screen showed four legs. Foxes again.

And then a scratch. A muffled bark. A whine.

Wait a minute.

He knew that whine. Surely not . . . ?

It couldn't be.

'*TG?*'

Ford slid open the door and was instantly knocked over. A bundle of excitement bounded in, stood on his chest and proceeded to almost lick him to death.

'TG! How are you, girl! Where have you *been*? Blimey . . . what's that terrible stink?

The pongy pooch sprang off him, ran back and pawed at the door, before stopping and turning back to Ford.

Fetch Fordo. Fordo. Fetch.

'Woof!' barked the dog. *Follow me.*

'Whoa . . . Hey, what's the rush? You've only just got here! Calm down and let me look at you . . .' And he banged the door shut.

The even-more-scruffy pooch jumped up at the door again, scratching and pawing desperately.

'Come here, girl. Let's get you some food.'

Follow me! Must follow me! Must follo—

Hold up . . . did he just say food?

Yes, Ford had wandered off to find some grub and antiseptic hand wash.

So after a quick slice of chicken pie, TG took charge. The dog saw what she was looking for. She bounded over to the games area and picked up . . . Stick! Buster's Stick! Oof! Heavy. She moved to the door and laid it down, facing outwards.

'Woof!'

'A baseball bat?' said Ford. 'TG, it's way too late for a game, girl.'

The dog lay down by the bat and whimpered. Then she looked straight up at Ford with her best imploring-eyes look.

'Wait a minute . . .' said Ford. 'Is it . . . ? It couldn't be.' He reached down and held the dog's head in his hands.

'TG . . . is it . . . Buster?'

If I have to wag this poor tail any harder, thought TG Dog, it'll fall off.

Ford Harrison grabbed his jacket and torch, flung open the door to BCHQ and ran out into the forest chasing one very smelly dog.

TG led him to where the pong came from. With 220 million scent receptors to a human boy's 5 million, she smelled it long before he did – but soon they were both standing near the exit to the sewer.

Ford put his hands on his knees then very quickly grabbed his nose. 'Phwoooouuuuuurrghhhh!'

The dog seemed to want him to . . . *follow her into the sewer?*

Then it dawned on him. The chink!

He took a deep – *eeaow*.

He took a shallow breath and considered. Could the dog have found the one way to get in undetected by cameras? No one would expect it. It was an exit, after all. And nobody would be expected to tolerate the almighty stench.

Nobody except someone who'd spent the past few months learning to live with Torsten Rodius, Guffmeister General. Who'd have thought his controversial open-border policy in the Republic of Trousania would ever come in useful?

So Ford followed the dog into the narrow tunnel. No footholds. Why would there be? Given what it was designed for, they'd just hold things up. He slipped. He slid. He tried to do it without hands, but only managed around two metres. Slowly does it. Thank heavens for antibacterial handwash. Mental note.

He scrambled up after the dog until at last he saw the light. *Aaaand* breathe. The things he did to save the world from evil.

The light was dazzling. It shone from huge lamps that swept the moat and bear pit. The dog timed her run between them.

He followed, at the right time, up to the fence – where TG found the hole, moved the twigs she'd laid there only hours before and disappeared.

Just what I need, thought Ford. Another tunnel.

This one, though, smelled pleasant by comparison – of earth, of warrens, of the roots of things. He crawled, less far this time, and emerged to find himself inside the impregnable defences – hearing not disappointed bears but a more rhythmic sound, coming from behind the nearby wall.

The *thump, bounce, thud* of someone throwing a baseball at a wall and catching it . . . Wait a minute . . .

'Buster!' he whispered. 'Is that you?'

Thump, bounce . . . nothing.

Disbelieving pause. Then, '. . . Fordo?'

'Buster! I can't believe it!'

'Fordo! Buddy! I knew you'd find a way. I just knew it . . .'

'It's so great to hear your voice! Are you okay? Have they hurt you? We'll get the cops! We'll bust this whole thing sky-high. We'll . . .'

'No cops!' stage-whispered the boy in the cell. 'They own the cops. They own the mayor. They own the radio station. They own everybody. You're Obi-Wan, buddy. My only hope.'

'But how do I get you out?'

'Use the race, Ford. It has to be the race. That's our window. You know about this weird white dude? The Stig?'

'Oh yeah, I know.'

'Okay, now listen. Cruiser's obsessed by him. It's all he

thinks about. So *if* he turns up to race – and PT's convinced he will – every camera in the place will be trained on him alone. That's it. That's the window. That's when you have to come for me.'

'But how do I break into your cell?'

'I've got that covered. There's a code on the door. *Beep-ba-ba-beep-ba . . . short pause . . . beep-ba-beep beep beep baa.'*

'Hold on, was that *Beep-ba or beep –*'

'You don't have to remember it! I remember it! Remember?'

'Yes, but you know – head start. Never mind, where were we?'

'You spring me during the race – and before it ends we pull the plug on Xenon. I know exactly how.'

'Great! How?'

'Like I said, we pull the plug.'

'Yeah, but how?'

'No, there's actually a really big plug that we have to pull.'

'What . . . a plug? Like, an actual –'

'Yeah, yeah, a really big one. What can I say? The guy's very literal.'

'That's settled then,' said Ford. 'I'll be back up here for you tomorrow, during the race. And we'll destroy Xenon first, then the whole Cruiser Corporation.' He was quiet for a second. 'Time for some payback.'

'You got it. And, Ford?

'Uh-huh?'

'I always knew you'd come through.'

If he only knew *what* I've just come through, thought Ford. But he just said, 'Hey, don't thank me. Thank TG.'

'Quick! I got company.'

'Okay. See you Saturday. For real.'

'Oh, and, Fordo? One more thing.'

Silence.

'Maybe think about taking a bath sometime? I can smell you from here. No offence, but . . . Ford? Ford?'

Ford, however, was already halfway to the fence.

'Hey, if your best friend won't tell you, who will?'

Silence.

'Ford? TG?'

Ah well. Plenty of time to tell him once he was out.

THIRTY-SIXTH: BUNSFOLD CALLING

In which we hear a special edition of the Radio X-NET Saturday Sports Show with your excitable hosts, Hal 'n' Hank

HAL: Hello again! The day of days is finally here. The hour of hours is upon us. The streets are lined with excited crowds, and the shopping-centre car park has been transformed into a race grid – it's a great big Bunsfold welcome to the show.

There are just MINUTES to go before the MASSIVE race, and sleepy Bunsfold is looking pretty WIDE AWAKE. Today is also the global launch of Xenon, of course, so we thought we'd get one of the Radio X-NET team to try it for himself – and who better than the never-lost-for-words Sidekick Sid.

So, Sid, tell us – just how good is Xenon?

Sid?

SID: With you in juuust . . . aaaa . . . sec . . .

HAL: 'Pretty tremendous' seems to be the verdict, if not exactly made for live radio. So let's go instead to Hank, who really is the pits. Sorry, in the pits. How's the atmosphere down there, Hank?

HANK: Awesome, Hal. Monaco, Indianapolis, Bunsfold, Le Mans: the world will soon have a new favourite motorsport event.

HAL: Who's your money on?

HANK: Well, Hal, there's a lot of extremely rich kids driving crazily expensive equipment, so it's not always easy to tell who's actually any good – but one kid at least has the natural talent to do her space-age kart justice. So it's hard to see past the local lass: the Blonde Bullet herself, Miss CC Cruiser.

HAL: Yup, that's where the smart money is – home advantage, and as we know she's heading the Corporation's fleet of Narnium karts. And if she's anything like her father, she'll be feeding off a competitive streak a mile wide. In a good way.

HANK: Chip off the old block, from everything I hear – she's definitely the one to beat. But Team Cruiser won't have it all their own way. With this level of prize money, the race has attracted the international Rich Brat Mafia – with extravagant karts and egos to match.

HAL: Yes, the young Russian Dollski is looking especially full of himself – but the French-Canadian kid Chevalnoir could be a dark horse. And from what I hear the Swede has a lot of people rooting for him . . .

HANK: Yes, and the Saudi outfit is a well-oiled machine, the Spanish team are feeling bullish, the Indian entry is fairly hot and, of course, you can never discount the Germans. It's all to play for. But it's hard to look past the young Cruiser kid to take the chequered flag in front of her home crowd – and with it the honour of pulling that lever.

HAL: Indeed, the global Xenon launch! We've all seen the pictures, queues around the block across the globe, but what about the actual game itself? Could it possibly be as awesome as people say? Sidekick Sid? Any comment on that?

Sid?

SID: Juust . . . ahhh . . .

HAL: He's hopping from foot to foot in a desperate attempt to avoid going to the toilet . . . and I'm taking that as a big positive.

And what a day to be launching this eighth wonder on the world, with TV crews from all the biggest gaming markets – sorry, proudest go-karting nations – on hand to cover it.

HANK: Yes, I imagine PT Cruiser will be pretty pumped. In a cool, almost statesmanlike way.

HAL: Did you know, Hank, that he gives absolutely DILLIONS away to good causes, but doesn't like to talk about it?

HANK: Wait, there's the five-minute warning, so it's time to go over to the grid and take a proper look at the field. Cabriola's on pole, with the Russian Dollski in second, looking like he can hardly contain himself. Meanwhile, back in last place are the other two members of the Cruiser Team in their distinctive all-black livery.

HAL: What do we know about those two identically dressed Team Narnium drivers, Hank? Paint me a picture.

HANK: Bit of an unknown quantity, Hal. They seem to move in perfect sync . . . almost robotic, you might say. The race card lists them simply as Kimi and Nigel Drone. We've googled them both and drawn a blank. So what do we think – they'll be protecting Cabriola as lead driver?

HAL: It'll be fascinating to find out, Hank. But what's that empty space at the back of the grid?

HANK: That was for the Bunsfold Rocket, the wild-card entry, taken by a pint-sized local lad called Ford Harrison. A modest boy with much to be modest about. But now he seems to have disappeared, so right now the wild card is looking like a busted flush. Shame.

Just time for a last word from our generous sponsor. It's beyond all imagining! It's all kinds of everything! It's . . .

Xenon fanfare & ad

THIRTY-SEVENTH

Start your engines

As Cabriola Cruiser sat at the front of the grid feeling the Narnium kart pulse beneath her, she was seized by the sensation that her whole life had led to this moment.

She felt herself move into the zone, that strange parallel universe she would enter just before the lights turned green. Crystalline focus. Complete calm. A sensation that the rest of the world was moving in slow motion. She was ready.

Until a familiar dillionaire's voice screeched over her helmet intercom.

'Cabriola. It's me. Your father. Do you Roger?'

The girl grimaced. 'I'm busy,' she said simply.

'Yes, I know,' said the voice. 'Copy. Over.'

'Whatever it is, this isn't the time.'

'I was just going to tell you that *he* still hasn't turned up . . .' said the voice. 'Can you believe this dude? I've gone to all this trouble to set the perfect trap, and –'

'I couldn't care less. Leave me to do my job,' said Cabriola. 'And one other thing. No cheats. No tricks. No games. Not this time. I'll win your race for you, PT Cruiser. But I'll do it my way. Over and out.'

She caught voices at the other end of the line. '*Maurice . . . I think she's gone. How do I turn this thing off . . . ?*'

The two-minute siren sounded, and the engineers, celebrities and TV reporters surrounding the karts instantly got out of the way.

One minute. The engines screamed.

Despite herself, Cabriola glanced in the mirror to check if The Stig had taken his place in the last kart.

No dice.

As they finished their final adjustments to the Rocket, Sam Wheeler, Ford Harrison and Minnie Cooper were each gripped by the sensation that their entire lives had led to this moment.

The three friends got to their feet and looked at each other. Then, without a word, they wheeled their curious contraption – part pram, part F1 car – to the last place on the grid.

Just ahead, the dark visors of the two all-black Cruiser-team drivers swivelled backwards in suspiciously exact unison, and fixed on them.

'We've done all we can,' said Sam as they walked back to the pits. 'Let's just pray he arrives.'

The two-minute siren blared.

'Strength and honour,' said Ford to them both. And he quietly checked the contents of his backpack for the third time. Torch. Check. Rubber gloves. Nose plugs. Deodorant spray. Check. Dog whistle inaudible to humans. Check.

'Hey – why so worried?' said Sam. 'I mean, you've only got

to break into an impregnable fortress, rescue your best friend and then save the world.'

Ford didn't smile, but scanned the horizon once again for any sign of The Stig.

Nothing.

One-minute warning.

Without another word Ford set his watch and turned to walk towards the forest.

Sam watched him shuffle away, two tiny shoulders carrying the weight of the world. What chance did he have? If The Stig failed to appear, and Cruiser's cameras and machine guns were undistracted, Ford would be walking straight into a firestorm.

And it had all been Sam's idea. He opened his mouth to call him back. Then closed it, silently.

'Stick with the plan, Wheels,' he said to himself. It was their only hope.

Though he had one other card to play. A card he'd kept secret even from Ford and Minnie. If the unthinkable happened, and The Stig failed to appear, he'd play it.

Minnie Cooper ran after Ford and tapped him on the shoulder. Then she leaned down – quite a way – and kissed him on the cheek. 'Hey. Still growing on me,' she said.

Ford blushed. Nodded. Walked on, towards his destiny.

Minnie turned back to the track, and, for the millionth time, willed The Stig to appear. 'He's got to come this time,' she said. 'He's just got to . . .'

*

At exactly the same time, the infinitely complex intelligence of the world's only Deathbot concluded that its entire existence had led to this moment.

Hiding in plain sight, the murderous machine scanned the race grid for any possible sign of **TARGET STIG**. And after once again processing all available inputs at approximately two dillion gigabytes a second, it reached the same conclusion.

TARGET PRESENCE IMMINENT.

Deep within its circuitry, a part of the machine contemplated its own imminent demise. For today would be the last day of its existence.

It accessed its memory bank.

Those delicious scientists. Chasing down the **TARGET VIRGIL BUSTER MUSTANG** in the forest. Shape-shifting into the teddy bear from *Toy Story 3*. **EMBARRASSING.**

And the **DOG.** How it wished it could have eaten the **DOG.**

It'd had a perfect opportunity once, but only in front of others, where its true identity would have been revealed.

But all this – and everything else – was about to end. Its mission was entirely specific. And it would end today.

MISSION OBJECTIVE:

TO FORCE TARGET STIG INTO CHAMBER OF COMBUSTION FOR TERMINATION OF STIG + DEATHBOT.

Just then, an **ALERT**.

A murder of crows wheeled up and away from some trees up in the forest surrounding MOTH.

STIG SIGN – STIG SIGN.

STAY CALM, DEATHBOT. COOL CIRCUITS. IT IS TIME.

The indescribably evil machine turned away from the race and, once out of sight, accelerated noiselessly towards the forest at the speed of a small family hatchback.

The race lights turned to red. The engines screamed.

Ten seconds to go.

Nine . . .

Eight . . .

Seven . . .

Six . . .

Five . . .

Quietly, and almost so you wouldn't notice, a white-suited racing driver strode towards to the Bunsfold Rocket and climbed in.

Four . . .

Three . . .

Two . . .

One . . .

The lights turned to green.

THIRTY-EIGHTH

In which the race is on

As the mysterious white racer strode out towards the Rocket, an eerie silence fell over the crowd. The watching world stopped and held its breath.

Cabriola Cruiser glanced in her mirrors and smiled grimly.

Why, Mr The Stig. We almost meet again.

At MOTH, PT Cruiser jumped a metre out of his seat and attempted to high-five the fist-pumping Maurice Marina.

It was *him*. A touch shorter than he remembered, but there was no mistaking that insolent – yet, he had to admit, strangely purposeful – stride.

And, high up in the stand, Gramps punched the air. He – and only he – knew who was really driving the Bunsfold Rocket.

And it wasn't The Stig.

He turned to Sam's mum and said simply, 'Now watch this boy go.'

She made the kind of 'reluctantly agreeing' noise kids make when told they have only five more minutes on the iPad before supper, and carried on playing.

Gently but firmly, Gramps prised the phone from his daughter's hands and said it again.

'Watch this boy.'

Meanwhile, every security camera, surveillance system, overstuffed black rubbish bin and black-suited henchman in Bunsfold swivelled in unison to focus on the Bunsfold Rocket.

'THREE . . . TWO . . . ONE . . .'

GREEN!

Bunsfold erupted in a shockwave as the ten most powerful and advanced karts ever built shot away from the line.

They looked like wheeled speed and sounded like the future. All apart from the Bunsfold Rocket, which resembled a pram with an old-fashioned desk fan stuck on the back and sounded like crockery in a cement mixer.

The karts surged past the grandstand in formation, led by the sinister matt black Narnium One driven by Cabriola Cruiser.

The mysterious white racer in the Bunsfold Rocket had taken a more leisurely approach. He limped away from the line with a kangaroo hop, and the rest of the field had already disappeared round the first bend by the time the hokey-looking kart had chugged into its stride.

All apart from the strangely robotic drivers of Narniums Two and Three, Kimi and Nigel Drone, who cruised down the straight just in front of the Rocket, watching its every move.

Up ahead, Cabriola Cruiser quickly opened an easy eight-second gap on the rest of the field, with the second-placed Russian Dollski getting smaller and smaller in her mirrors.

She was now deep in the zone, driving with a supernatural

touch down a course she'd raced hundreds of times on MOTH's life-size simulator. It was as if she was accelerating into an endless tunnel, where time and space –

Another screech on her helmet intercom.

'Er . . . PT calling Narnium One. Come in, Narnium One.'

'Narnium One to base,' she replied. 'No time to chat. Do you read?'

'Yes. Mainly magazines and the odd paperback. Nothing heavy. But that's not important right now. Just wanted to let you know that Mr The Stig turned up after all . . . so it's all okay. You can just go and win now. But slow down a bit first, will you? You're making the others look bad.'

'*Slow down?*'

'Yes. All these kids are from major Xenon markets, Narnium One, so let's make a game of it.'

'I told you. My way or not at all. Staying at Maximum Attack.'

'No, Narnium One. Switch to . . . Minimum Attack.'

'No can do.'

'Now hold your horses there for a moment, please, Narnium One. Let's just remember what I'm offering here, shall we? Dillion-dollar salary? Leaving school for ever, right now? The hand of Liam from One Direction?'

'The *hand*?'

'Arm, leg, whichever bit you want. Talk to Sergei and he'll sort something out. Now . . . do you want all this or not?'

Cabriola was silent.

PT went on. 'I can't hear you?'

'YES. I WANT IT ALL.' She petulantly hit the KILL INTERCOM button and throttled back the kart. Then two last words, for her own ears alone: 'I think.'

Immediately, the tiny Russian Dollski in her mirrors turned into a slightly larger version – and continued getting bigger every time she looked.

Meanwhile, at the very back of the race, the Bunsfold Rocket was only trundling. As it chugged through the tricky Hammerhead corner – recently renamed after PT Cruiser's favourite pet – it was stuck firmly in last place.

High up in the stands, Sam's mum gazed, blinking, into the distance, her hands shaking. 'This Stig bloke's not terribly good, is he? Why's he going so slowly?'

Gramps was quiet. He'd considered telling Mrs W who was *really* driving the Bunsfold Rocket, but in her present condition she might not take the news well. It was bad enough he'd only been able to persuade one parent to attend. But all that was, he hoped, about to change.

'He's getting a feel for the kart,' he said simply.

'Well, he'd better get a feel quickly,' said Mrs Wheeler, 'or he's toast.'

At least she's paying attention, thought Gramps.

But as the Rocket went past them for the second time the white-suited driver at the helm finally stepped on it and found some proper speed down the straight.

He slipstreamed right up behind the two black Cruiser

Narnium karts immediately ahead, and they magically parted – one to the left, one to the right – and, in suspiciously exact unison, waved him through the gap they'd left in between.

'Wait a minute . . .' said Gramps, eyes widening. 'No . . . NO!'

As the Bunsfold Rocket accelerated into the gap, the heads of the black kart drivers each miraculously extended from their bodies, like insect eyes on stalks, and swivelled ninety degrees to face the white-suited driver.

Gramps got to his feet and screamed, 'NOW! HIT THE BUTTON NOW!'

At that exact second, almost as if he'd heard him, a white-gloved finger reached down towards the control panel of the Bunsfold Rocket and pushed a switch labelled – in Ford Harrison's dodgy handwriting – HYPERDRIVE.

There was a rumble, then a surge, then a noise like a thousand vacuum cleaners as the giant fan-supercharger on the back of the kart whirred into life. And the second it did, the Bunsfold Rocket catapulted through the gap as if fired from a bazooka.

Just as two green laser beams shot from the helmets of the murderous Cruiser Drone drivers into the now-empty gap between them, succeeding only in slicing each other's robotic heads clean off.

Inside the Bunsfold Rocket, a white-suited Sam Wheeler shouted to himself. '*Ford Harrison*,' he yelled as the Rocket hurtled down the track after the leaders, '*you legend*.'

It had been Gramps's idea to bring Sam a mini-Stig disguise, just in case. In fact, the old man had spent all night painting an

old black motorcycle helmet white. Or rather 'Magnolia', since that was the only paint he could find in the garage.

Maurice Marina put his hand over his eyes in anticipation of his not-famously-tolerant boss's reaction. But PT Cruiser was cool.

'Don't worry, Maurice,' he said. 'I have just the thing to stop our Mr Smarty-Stig dead in his tracks.'

'I'm not sure anything can stop him, boss. You know what he's like when he gets the bit between his teeth.'

'Oh, don't worry, Maurice. What I've arranged will most definitely do the trick. You'll see. Stick around. Our taciturn friend is about to be beaten . . . by a twelve-year-old girl! Ha!'

Just then something strange began to happen.

A crack of thunder, audible over the roar of engines.

Jet-black clouds rolled across the sky towards the track like an oily tarpaulin.

There was menace in the air.

And way up in the hills over Bunsfold – right where the Mansion On The Hill sat staring darkly down at the town – jagged bolts of forked lightning lit the sky.

'What on *earth* is happening?' said Mrs W to Gramps as raindrops the size of sherbet lemons pounded the track. 'I've never seen the like. I suppose they'll have to stop the race.'

The old man wiped the water from his face.

'Oh no, they won't stop,' he said. 'Don't you see? This isn't just a race.' And he turned to stare at her in the darkness.

'It's a Reckoning.'

THIRTY-NINTH

In which Ford Harrison stars in . . . Mission Impossible

Just moments after he'd set off into the forest towards MOTH, Ford stopped behind some bushes, opened his backpack and pulled out the silent dog whistle.

He hadn't arranged a rendezvous with TG: that's not how it works with dogs. But he was still surprised – and a bit thrown – when she didn't turn up.

And suddenly he felt very alone.

He looked all the way up the hill to where the Cruiser Mansion glowered down at him. 'Have a go,' it seemed to say, 'if you think you're hard enough.'

He wasn't sure he *was* hard enough.

He thought of his best friend, Buster, imprisoned in the mansion. He thought of the time he'd glimpsed the insane, addictive power of Xenon, and what it would do to the world. He thought of all those endless nights alone in BCHQ, plotting to find a way – any way – to stop the dark forces in Bunsfold. He thought of Minnie – his extraordinary, adorable Minnie – and the iced teas she'd been having with his friend Sam. And he felt the weight of the world on his slender shoulders.

Suddenly it all felt too much. He began to sob, silently.

Pull yourself together, Ford. Focus.

Think of your buddy, Ford. Mustang.

Just then, he heard the quiet hum of a surveillance camera in a nearby tree . . . then another, in an overstuffed black rubbish bin further up the path. Startled, he ducked down behind the bushes and made himself as small as possible – which was pretty small.

But the cameras hadn't turned towards him. They'd both swivelled simultaneously to some unseen point in the distance – and he knew exactly where.

Bunsfold Race Track.

Bingo, thought Ford.

Buster had been right. The mystery white-suited driver had finally shown himself, and for now all the Cruiser Corporation's eyes were trained on him.

He had his window.

He wiped his eyes angrily and slipped between the cameras towards the Pipe of Doom.

When he finally arrived at the entrance to the sewer, there was still no mongrel to be seen. Well, he couldn't wait for her.

Below him he could hear the wail of engines, and smell the whiff of hot oil and smoking brakes.

If only, he thought, he could keep smelling it for ever. Not that it was especially pleasant. It just wasn't an actual sewer. He reached into his pack for the nose plugs, pulled on the gloves, checked his watch, had one last look for the dog and began the ascent alone.

Six malodorous minutes and seventeen stinky seconds later, he emerged, blinking, into the daylight. Ford prayed that Buster's theory about the cameras remained true here as well – that PT Cruiser's Stig override meant any possible sighting trumped all other considerations.

He ripped off the gloves, sprayed himself all over with the scent of 'Ocean Gale' and sprinted across to the wall of Buster's cell without getting lasered. So far so good.

Now to get inside. He knew the plans by heart. He'd memorised the route. All the same, he was pleased to see the sign saying THIS WAY TO THE CELL BLOCKS, and a neon arrow pointing round to the left.

No guards. No sentries. No bears. That was the genius of the sewer route. Its disadvantages were there for all to smell, but, on balance, he'd take a bit of social embarrassment over a hungry grizzly.

Sam had been right. There is *always* a chink.

Five minutes later he found himself tiptoeing along the high-security corridor of Cell Block A, listening hard.

There it was – the telltale sound he'd been hoping for. *Thump, bounce, thud.* He knocked. The bouncing stopped.

'Fordo?' called Buster from inside. 'Bang on time!'

'The code! Quick!' whispered Ford through the door.

'*Beep-ba-beep-beep-ba . . .*'

Ford pushed the buttons, getting *Beep-ba-beep-beep-ba . . .* damn. Seems the three goes ba, not beep. Try again . . . *Beep-ba-ba-beep-ba . . . beep-ba-beep beep beep . . .*

And *baa*! The door sprang open.

He was finally face to face with his best friend.

The two stood opposite each other in silence. Then Buster smiled. 'Not bad, Ford. Not bad at all.'

Then he parked the touching reunion scene for later and strode out of the door.

A tall and authoritative figure stepped forward from the corner of the cell. Ford's back instinctively straightened.

'Sir!' he said.

'Harrison,' said the headmaster. 'Extraordinary. The only pupil in the history of Bunsfold High to score zero in the science examination, and you break into this place.'

'Okay,' interrupted Buster. 'Save it for later, guys. Let's do this.'

'Do what, exactly?' said the Head. 'If it's anything other than "get the police", I'm afraid I can't allow it.'

'Headmaster,' said Buster, 'I've enjoyed our time together. The chess, the respect for each other's space, the lessons in pre-Napoleonic French agriculture. And not mentioning the baseball cap on the tower was classy. But all good things come to an end. As for the cops, PT Cruiser owns them. Same goes for the radio station, the mayor and the stupid traffic wardens. You'd have to go and get police from outside Bunsfold, but the roads are shut for the race and we don't have much time. Happy for you to make a run for it and see what whistles you can blow, but Ford and I have to do this ourselves. Sir.'

The Head took this in, nodded, made a decision.

'Very well. Good luck. And don't worry. I'll be back with help. Count on it.'

'Good luck yourself, sir,' said Buster, and after a quick and respectful handshake with his cellmate the Head ducked down and headed for the woods.

As the boys ran out into the compound, there was a blinding jag of lightning, then, almost instantaneously, a deafening thunderclap. Raindrops the size of wine gums spattered their faces.

They sprinted through the rain towards the buggy. Stretched out ahead of them – as big as several football pitches – was the vast MOTH compound.

Ford glanced at his watch. 'The race will be finishing any second, so we don't have long,' he said. 'We've got to get over to Cruiser's lair. Think you can find it?'

'No problem,' said Buster calmly. 'How do you start these things?'

'Red button,' said Ford. 'Says STARTER on it.'

'Worth a shot,' agreed Buster.

He pushed. Nothing. Zilch. *Nada.*

He pushed again. Same result.

'The henchmen must have electronic chips on their uniforms,' he said. 'That Maurice guy just got in and drove it.'

Buster hit the steering wheel with frustration.

Now what?

FORTIETH

In which we watch the race, Part Two

As soon as the rain began to lash horizontally across Bunsfold, the magnolia-helmeted driver of the Bunsfold Rocket finally found his race pace. Now there were giant puddles all over the track, and his ugly but mightily nimble kart started to scythe through the field.

Sam was a competition cyclist, not a go-kart driver, and the Rocket had taken some getting used to, but when he calmed himself down and relaxed the speed began to ratchet up. Smoothness, it seemed, was the key. And now he was clipping every corner, dancing through the turns and using the Rocket's miraculous Fan-Kart grip to maximum effect.

The gap to the front was closing. Fast.

With the Rocket all over his back bumper, the fairly hot Indian soon lost his cool and spun out at Chicago. Young Chevalnoir was eating grass in no time and the Russian Dollski came apart after aquaplaning straight into the tyre wall at Gambon. The Saudi kid found oil and water didn't mix, the Spaniard gored the tyre wall and the Swede blew a tyre of his own and got mashed.

Just two karts left. Just two laps to go.

Cabriola Cruiser glanced once more in her mirrors and caught sight of the one thing she'd been expecting. And, in some strange way, the thing she'd most wanted.

The Stig.

Or so she thought.

She hit the helmet intercom. 'Switching to Maximum Attack.'

'Permission granted, Narnium One. See you on the victory parade.'

Cabriola smiled grimly in her helmet. Finally she could unleash Narnium One's full power down the back straight. Ha! Instantly the plucky but very home-made Bunsfold Rocket disappeared in a cloud of spray, and Narnium One surged away into the awkward left-right combination the villagers knew as the Bunsfold Recreation Ground Footpath.

As she disappeared into the distance – towards victory, towards her destiny – Cabriola Cruiser turned to mock the absurd contraption left straggling in her wake.

But, peering into the wall of water thrown up by her own giant rear tyres, her grin evaporated. Because coming out of the spray behind her was the ugly, lopsided grille of a small but lovingly constructed home-made go-kart, and a mysterious white-suited driver who clearly didn't understand that he was beaten.

Back in the best seat in the stadium, the shifty dillionaire PT Cruiser turned to his top henchman, Maurice Marina.

'Initiate Plan Death Race 2000, Maurice.'

The henchman looked uncomfortable. 'You absolutely sure, boss? I mean, it is a bit . . . well . . . *dark* of us. The eyes of the world and all that.'

PT shot him a look that said, 'You could be fired any second, you muppet. Now get on with it or you'll be swimming with the fishes. For about ten seconds.'

Maurice gulped. He'd seen the piranhas in action and removed their leftovers from the tank personally. It never took long.

He initiated the Plan.

One lap to go, and the Bunsfold Rocket was now right on the giant rear aerofoil of Narnium One. It feinted once to the left . . . then, just lightly, to the left again.

A memory stirred in the back of Cabriola's head. A memory of the new kid Wheeler overtaking her in the forest. It was exactly the same move he'd pulled that night.

He's bluffing, she thought to herself. He's going to duck right.

She was right.

Cabriola dived to block the move, exactly as the chasing Rocket swung that way to pass her. She'd left him nowhere to go.

Now they were on the endless straight that stretched the length of Xenfield car park, where Narnium One could use all of its astonishing turbo power to open up a five . . . six . . . seven . . . second gap.

Finally she arrived at the toughest and most dangerous corner of the track.

The Follow-Through.

Far away from the grandstand, and quite invisible to any spectator or TV camera, was a treacherous blind humpback in the road that sent the karts flying into the air with no idea what they'd find on the other side.

Narnium One arrived at maximum attack – too fast, *surely* – took off at top speed, landed just the other side of a giant slick of oily water, then instantly flicked its tail sideways to make the sharp left turn ahead.

High up in the grandstand, Gramps nodded in appreciation of an astonishing piece of skill. Bullying brat or not, this Cabriola kid had what it took.

After a seemingly endless gap, Sam finally arrived at the same blind humpback.

The Bunsfold Rocket launched into the air at maximum speed, with no idea what awaited.

How could he have known anything? How could anyone?

Because right there, pushed into the middle of the road and tied to a trolley, lay a scruffy, wounded and terrified mongrel.

And the kart was flying straight at her.

As the Rocket hit the track, throwing sparks high into the air, Sam feathered the brakes and instantaneously swerved right to avoid her.

Towards the one obstacle every racing driver fears above all others.

Trees.

With no thought for his own welfare, he accelerated to miss

TG by a scruffy whisker and hurtled straight on towards the oaks of Bunsfold Forest.

Everything was happening in slow motion. Sam looked down at his legs, and wondered what they'd look like after impact. His short life passed before his eyes . . . his mum leaning over him lovingly as he lay in a cot . . . his tiny hand reaching out of a pram to release the brake . . . Gramps teaching him to ride a bike . . . racing Cabriola through the rain . . .

Then, right in front of him, a dream-vision. It was The Stig. And the white racer was gesturing to him.

Release the steering wheel.

Fold your arms.

Sam did so just as the Rocket skidded across the wet grass straight towards the trunk of an ancient oak.

He closed his eyes and braced for impact.

Whuuummmmp.

Sam opened one eye.

Just before he'd smashed into the tree, a giant Cruiser Corporation inflatable airbag had exploded out of the grass right in front of the Rocket.

Now he was wrapped in giant folds of squidgy foam rubber.

Instantly, black-suited henchmen emerged to surround the kart and whisk away the chained mutt. Screens were erected in seconds to hide the crash scene.

PT Cruiser turned to Maurice. 'I can't bear to look,' he said. 'Tell me . . . is he alive?'

'Alive,' said Maurice. 'More's the pity.'

'Yeeeeesssssss!' said PT, punching the sky.

Maurice looked perplexed. 'Boss . . . do you want this geezer six feet under or don'tcha? I'm a little confused.'

PT composed himself. 'It's complicated.'

'Oh, I geddit,' replied his loyal henchman. 'Sort of a hopeless man-crush thing, eh?'

PT went purple, then calmed himself. 'Maurice, my relationship with my nemesis is complex. Yes, a part of me would very much like to see him atomised in a giant nuclear combustion chamber of my own design. But then another part of me suspects that without him life would be empty. And that I would be simply one hand clapping.'

Maurice looked blank. PT went on.

'Now, let me enjoy Project Daughter's victory. Then I and Mr The Stig will finally have a chance to talk. I have questions for him, you see. So many, many questions.'

Meanwhile, the crowd knew none of this. They were too busy watching the race leader take the final bend of a legendary victory.

With The Rocket no longer visible in her mirrors, and entirely unaware of the dirty doggy dealings that had occurred behind her, Cabriola throttled back and drove calmly down towards the chequered flag.

She caught the looks of crazed idolatry on the faces of the Xenon-addicted fans who were lining the straight.

She thought of the dillion-dollar salary, the fame and the

glory that would now be hers for ever.

She contemplated pulling, in just a moment or two, the really big lever that would launch on a waiting world the greatest computer game ever devised.

She was just a few metres short of the line now. The last kart standing in a ferocious, once-in-a-lifetime race.

As she looked up, she saw the fatherly pride in the eyes of PT Cruiser, his arms outstretched towards her. For this had been his victory too, of course.

She looked deeper into those wild eyes. Closed in on the manic grin. Heard the crowd chant, '*Xe-non! Xe-non! Xe-non!*' Felt the rush of admiration. Took a breath. And then, just ten metres short of the finish . . .

She stopped dead.

The crowd gasped.

Cabriola Cruiser had indeed found her destiny. But it was a different destiny from the one her father had planned.

She climbed out of the kart and removed her helmet. Silence fell across Bunsfold, and then the world.

She looked up at PT.

'I could have won, Dad,' she said. And she paused for a moment. 'But tell me, what would it prove?'

And she turned and walked towards her trusty Narnium BMX, sitting waiting by the side of the track.

She threw the bike into a 360-degree tail whip and wheelied away.

Into a whole new future.

FORTY-FIRST

In which the white (/magnolia) helmet is finally removed

PT Cruiser was boiling with rage.

First, his daughter (how he choked on the word) had utterly disobeyed him. She was dead to him now.

Second, there was *no winner* of the greatest kart race in history, the Bunsfold TT.

So now who would pull the really big red lever he'd had set up by the podium to launch his masterpiece globally?

Billions of people who were just crying out to be hopelessly manipulated were now left hanging.

There was, of course, one compensation for all this. And it was not a minor one.

He had *him*.

Finally. He had caught The Stig.

As he strode down towards the crash scene on the edge of the forest, he felt, in some strange way he couldn't quite understand, that his whole life had led to this moment.

He turned to his henchman, Maurice Marina.

'Maurice. Since the dawn of time, mankind has sought answers to the Three Great Questions of Life.' He paused for a moment.

'First, is there a God? Second . . . why are we here? And third . . . who is The Stig? And today PT Cruiser will answer one of those questions. For all time.'

He stopped in front of the makeshift curtains erected around the crash scene. He straightened out his onesie and ran his hand over the sticky-out bits of hair at the sides of his bald head.

He was ready.

He parted the curtains.

When he first glimpsed his nemesis sitting calmly by the side of the stricken Bunsfold Rocket, he almost fainted with anticipation.

Maurice guided his boss gently to a makeshift seat that had been placed directly opposite – but higher than – that of the White Racer.

Finally, PT spoke. There was a quiver in his voice.

'So. Mr The Stig. I have relished the prospect of this moment for some time.'

The driver was silent. PT found himself gazing deeply into a dark visor that seemed to mirror his very soul.

'We have so much to discuss, Mr The Stig. Allow me to introduce myself. I am PT Cruiser.'

Still the driver said nothing.

'Though some describe me as the greatest scientific mind and dillionaire of our age, I prefer to go by the simple moniker of "computer man". You see, in many ways, despite my manifest greatness, in my head I'm still that simple, geeky kid I always was, quietly coding away on his own in his bedroom with no friends and dubious personal hygiene.'

Still The Stig was silent.

'But forgive me – you must think me rude. Let me offer you a drink. Some say you have a preference for high-octane petrol, and that you take it straight from the nozzle. So I've taken the liberty of sourcing this rather satisfactory bottle of BP Unleaded. It's the '97.'

Still, the driver was having none of it.

'Come, come, Mr The Stig. You disappoint me. We are really not so different, you and I . . .'

And then, finally . . . it happened.

For the first time in history.

The Stig . . . *spoke.*

'I could murder a Wagon Wheel, if there's one going spare . . .'

PT Cruiser, Maurice Marina and eighty-eight black-suited henchmen stood with mouths agape.

Eventually, PT replied.

'Tell me, please, that someone got that on film.'

The eccentric dillionaire shook with anticipation. You can't eat a Wagon Wheel with a helmet on. Simply can't be done. So the moment had arrived. It was time to remove it.

He beckoned Maurice forward.

The henchman silently unfastened the sacred chinstrap. Then, with great reverence, ever-so-gently lifted the helmet free . . . to find . . .

A long-haired kid with specs.

'WHAT?' shrieked PT. 'SAMUEL WHEELER?'

'Sorry, Cruiser,' said the boy, 'but you've been punked. I'm afraid the real Stig didn't show up after all, so I took the liberty of stepping in.'

Now the not famously-good-at-getting-bad-news dillionaire looked fit to explode.

'So . . . where is HE? Mr The REAL Stig?'

And just then – just exactly then – his question was answered. From far up in the hills surrounding Bunsfold, an unmissable siren screeched.

All eyes turned upwards towards the lights flashing from every corner of the MOTH.

It was the Stig alarm. From the Mansion On The Hill.

PT Cruiser realised he'd been duped.

While he'd been fooling around watching kids in go-karts, his nemesis had broken into his own back yard.

'Maurice!' he yelled. 'Prepare the helicopter gunship!' He shot an evil glance at Sam. 'And the piranha tank.'

Sam gulped, and steeled himself.

PT had taken the bait. Now, finally, he was about to enter the Monster's Lair.

FORTY-SECOND

In which there are fifty-nine seconds to save the world

Buster thumped the buggy's steering wheel in frustration. 'We're running out of time, Fordo. There's no way we can get across to Cruiser's Lair on foot before they arrive.'

Just then, as they sat there in stumped silence surveying the World's Most Dangerous Obstacle Course stretched out before them, something very strange began to happen.

From the forest beyond the walls of MOTH, a huge flock of black birds rose, startled, into the air and wheeled towards them.

Then, in between cracks of thunder, came the distant strains of a faraway lullaby played on rusty bagpipes. And it was coming from the sewer pipe.

Over by the entrance they could just make out a lone figure standing in the gloom.

Its arms were crossed and it stood with legs apart. Staring, silently, straight at them. Ford glimpsed a white helmet.

A bolt of lightning jagged down and illuminated the end of the pipe.

It was *him*.

'It's The . . .' said Ford.

'. . . Stig,' said Buster. The two boys stared at the figure in shock.

Miraculously, given where he'd just been, the new arrival was still white-suited, with not a single worrying splodge anywhere on him.

Another fork of lightning cracked overhead, before striking downwards to hit the white helmet.

Not a flinch.

The Stig strode straight over to the buggy and nodded towards the driver's seat, his suit still smoking from the lightning strike. Buster moved over without a word.

A white-gloved hand flipped up the battery panel of the buggy and stuck a crackling finger into its socket. There were sparks and a *whirr-rr-rr* of motors. The Stig leaned in as if reassuring a nervous horse. The little engine purred eagerly into life and the kart trundled away across the MOTH complex.

The Stig siren screamed louder. And back down at the track PT Cruiser and his henchmen climbed aboard his personal helicopter gunship.

As the buggy raced on across the compound, they could hear rumbling V8 engines. Then they saw them – two black vans, approaching from both sides.

Buster, for one, knew what was coming. They had three minutes, tops.

The helicopter gunship rose in the sky.

Make that two minutes.

Last time, with Maurice driving him, it had taken that long just to skirt round the bear pit. This time, though, the driver took a different line.

He was heading straight for it! They were close enough to . . . WHOA!

The buggy drove straight into the pit, as if dropping into a skateboard bowl.

Right ahead of them were the two biggest and angriest specimens of *Ursus arctos horribilis* any of them had ever seen. But instead of dropping to the floor of the pit, the driver wrenched the wheel left and took the buggy round the sheer side of the bowl like a motorbike on a Wall of Death.

The boys clung on for dear life – not a metaphor – as the sideways buggy somehow gripped the sides, gathering more and more momentum. The bears swiped, missed, roared, and finally became too dizzy to stand as the driver wrenched the wheel the other way and launched the tiny vehicle up into the air and out of the pit.

Right towards the radioactive moat.

The drawbridge was still down. They hadn't even bothered to raise it when the entire operation decamped to the race. SO cocky.

But from his fast-approaching helicopter gunship a nutty dillionaire in a black onesie was watching everything unfold. He shouted to Maurice to pass him his huge remote control. On it were two really big buttons saying RAISE DRAWBRIDGE and DROP PORTCULLIS ON STIG'S HELMET. He started hitting them both very hard over and over again while shouting terrible things.

The drawbridge began to rise. The portcullis began to fall.

But the white racer was driving at Maximum Attack, because for him there is no other kind.

He bounced the buggy once, pulled back on the steering wheel and the modest machine took off, clamping its front wheels on to the edge of the drawbridge. With three on board, it was heavy enough to pull the bridge back down to ground level.

Somehow finding hidden horsepower in the guts of the tiny engine, the driver coaxed the buggy across. The wood was soaking from the rain, and more slippery than an ice rink. As the portcullis began to fall like a slow-motion guillotine, the driver steered into the skid.

Instinctively the two young passengers shifted all their weight the same way – and forced the buggy into a four-wheel drift that took them right underneath the razor-sharp underside of the descending metal gate. Two of them ducked. The other didn't bother. Ford gave silent thanks that Project High Hair still had teething troubles. The portcullis slammed shut.

They were safely inside!

Not *that* safely. The out-of-control buggy was now spinning at full speed towards the unlit piranha tank!

As they hurtled towards their fishy fate, The Stig calmly reached down, turned on the buggy's radio and tuned in to a documentary on Colombian storage jars.

'Piranhas!' yelled Buster, shoving Ford out of the kart. He tumbled out and rolled before coming to an ungainly rest millimetres from the edge of the tank. Buster did the same. The white-suited driver chose the more elegant option of staying right where he was as the buggy plunged in.

The water filled with the sound of frantic fins and gnashing teeth.

Oh no, thought each boy independently. We're sunk.

But then.

There was a gurgling roar from beneath the surface as the buggy rose up, much like an elderly Poseidon's powered wheelchair, and landed on the side. The white figure strode out and on towards the lair, a flapping carnivorous fish clamped firmly to each buttock.

The boys looked at each other. It wasn't just that he was totally unharmed. He wasn't even wet.

The Stig strode on, no satnav required. He seemed to know exactly where he was going.

At last they were at the door to the lair.

And behind them, over the roar of the thunderstorm, they heard a helicopter gunship land in the compound.

FORTY-THIRD

In which we enter the dragon's den

PT Cruiser's helicopter gunship was landing just behind him. The future of mankind was at stake. But as he stood facing the security panel of the dillionaire's lair, Buster Mustang stayed eerily calm.

This was payback time. He'd memorised the door code to the inner sanctum so intensely that it had become a permanent earworm, present and correct no matter what the pandemonium around him. He pressed the numbers on the touch screen.

Beep-ba-ba-beep-ba . . . beep-ba-beep beep beep baa.

A sign flashed up.

LEVEL ONE COMPLETE.

There are *levels*?

Now a different, much larger screen appeared. And, from a hatch underneath, two hand-controllers.

Of course, thought Buster. To make it into the private lair of arch-gamer PT Cruiser you were going to have to play one of his games. Play and win.

The screen instantly transformed into a virtual battle scene of burnt-out buildings, wrecked cars and civilians. Occasionally, a virtual Cruiser Corporation henchman would duck out from behind a bombed tank and fire a green laser beam right at you. Buster and Ford looked at each other. They'd have to learn the controls, find out who to shoot and get it right first time without getting shot themselves.

Easy with a bit of practice; very hard in no time flat with the whirr of blades from a twin-rotor helicopter gunship right behind you. Turns out those things are *really* loud up close.

'He's playing a game with us,' said Buster, 'and we've lost all our lives.' For the first time since he'd fallen to the forest floor all those months ago, his shoulders slumped.

Then The Stig stepped forward. He looked up at the game screen. He looked down at the controllers. He selected one and held it to his helmet where an ear would be. He shook it, as if listening. He put it down. He walked away, back down the corridor.

Then he climbed into the buggy and drove off.

Great, thought Ford and Buster. When the going gets tough, The Stig disappears. It seemed they were on their own after all. They picked up a controller each. They just might get lucky.

Who were they kidding? This was a PT special – a game that started at a level higher than mere mortals could pick up. And who wanted to play computer games at a time like this? They were trying to save the world from being enslaved by one. Still, they forced themselves to concentrate.

It was no good. In the first ten seconds they scored eight

deaths, zero kills. And each time the virtual Cruiser henchman shot them with his green laser beam, the controller would send a progressively more painful electric shock up each arm.

Ford dropped his controller. The pain was becoming unbearable. Mankind's future wasn't looking good.

All of a sudden there was a break in the incessant noise. The sirens paused for breath. The helicopter rotors came to rest with a slow *whump . . . whuuump . . . whuuuuump*. The boys heard feet hitting the ground in the distance.

Meanwhile, some way behind them, the mysterious white-suited race driver had turned the tiny buggy back round. Now it was facing Buster, and Ford, and the door to the lair.

The Stig put on his tiny seatbelt. He revved the tiny engine. Then he tooted the tiny horn.

Parp parp.

Ford and Buster looked round.

The buggy was driving straight at them.

They threw themselves to the side. Just in time.

The Stig hurtled past, smashed straight through the screen and crashed through the wall behind it.

The boys followed through the dust. Behind them, heavy footsteps thudded in pursuit.

Finally they were inside the lair. And for a moment they froze.

Straight ahead of them was a massive, thundering machine covering the whole wall. A giant cylindrical mechanism breathtaking in its scope and majesty: the nightmarish Chamber of Combustion. A dark red light pulsed from it now. A low, throbbing rumble of readiness filled the room. It was an engine whose moment had come.

The Stig stepped out of the wrecked buggy, dusted himself down and strode straight towards the giant red plug helpfully labelled GLOBAL XENON SUPERBRAIN (SUBJUGATION OF MANKIND).

Just as an enigmatic dillionaire walked through the buggy-shaped hole in the wall.

The Stig turned to face him, and crossed his arms.

PT Cruiser trembled. This was *him*. Oh yes, no doubt about it. No doubt at all.

He took a deep breath and composed himself. Then, finally – after years of preparation and countless teams of scriptwriters – he delivered the short, ironic and relentlessly polished sentence he'd been dreaming of saying for years.

'NOT SO FAST, STIG!'

PT Cruiser strode into the room. Behind him, Maurice escorted a white-suited and serious-looking Sam Wheeler.

PT pulled a really big security remote control from his pocket and pressed a large button labelled SEAL THE LAIR.

Instantly, the buggy-shaped hole in the wall began to disappear before their eyes.

Narnium, thought Sam to himself as the hole magically closed up, trapping them all inside. Here, on the edge of oblivion.

Silence. The dark red pulsing light from the Chamber of

FORTY-FOURTH

Showdown

The offer was met with silence – although, to be fair, Ford did look interested.

PT addressed the room.

'Very well. First, allow me to congratulate you, Mr Samuel Wheeler, and Mr Ford Harrison, and Mr Buster Mustang. You have brought me the one thing I most craved. The . . . The –'

'The Stig,' interrupted Maurice.

'YES, YES, I KNOW HIS NAME, MAURICE, THANK YOU!' said PT. 'I was pausing for effect.'

The Stig turned to the Chamber of Combustion and stood facing it, as if transfixed.

'Mr The Stig. For many years you and I have teased, tantalised and tormented one another. But now, finally, the time has come. The time to reveal your true . . . your true –'

A buzz on the intercom.

'Oh, for heaven's SAKE,' said PT. 'What is it now? Can't a guy get fifteen lousy minutes to monologue at his nemesis?'

He looked up to the bank of screens covering the right-hand wall, where an anonymous henchman was marching an unusually tall girl with short hair towards the lair.

'Minnie!' said Sam and Ford.

PT Cruiser's intercom crackled.

'Found her in the woods, boss, making her way up here. Thought you'd like to see her in person.'

'Nothing I'd like more,' said PT, his black eyes shining moistly in the dark red light.

The door opened with a barely audible *szzzzzzjjoup* and the girl was marched into the room.

'Welcome, Miss Minnie Cooper,' said PT. 'We've been expecting you. In fact, we've been expecting you *especially*.'

Minnie looked pale, though not frightened. Then again, she didn't scare easily.

She smiled weakly at Sam and Ford, then stared, silently, at the back of The Stig as he stood absolutely still, facing the Chamber of Combustion.

'Leave her out of this, Cruiser,' said Sam, staring at PT with an intensity that made the dillionaire gulp.

'You lay a hand on her, and I swear –' said Ford.

But PT – who had quickly composed himself – interrupted him. 'My dear Mr Harrison. From the few short minutes you spent playing Xenon, I am already aware of the depth of your feelings for the fragrant Miss Cooper. The lengthy poems. The hydraulic shoe-lifts. The elaborately planned hot dates to racy archaeology conferences. So I'm sorry to inform you that the short life of your you-wish girlfriend will shortly be . . . *terminated*. Here. Tonight. In the Chamber of Combustion.'

And he paused to allow the shock of his words to sink in. 'Just as soon as I finish my monologue.'

Sam, Ford and Buster looked at him, appropriately shocked. And just then . . .

Up on the giant bank of screens directly behind PT's head . . . a fleet of what looked like . . . police vans appeared. Arriving in the MOTH compound.

Then an armoured personnel carrier.

Then police cars. But not Bugattis and mid-engined Ferraris. Cars that looked as if they'd had a few criminals in them. Ford Mondeos.

Sam caught Ford's eye, and nodded silently towards the screen.

Now they could see black-suited henchmen being slapped into handcuffs and marched into police cars, and wheel clamps being rammed on to sinister black vans. Two giant grizzly bears sat quietly in the back seat of a panda car, clearly resigned to their fate.

The cavalry had arrived. And at its head? The Head, of course.

Buster Mustang spotted his distinguished cellmate marching ahead of the police and SWAT team now pouring into MOTH And he was giving all the instructions – because *everyone* does what a headmaster tells them.

Oblivious to everything silently unfurling on the screens behind him, PT Cruiser resumed his monologue.

'Now . . . Mr The Stig. Forgive me. Where was I? Ah yes . . .

In many ways, we are fighting the same war. A war to provide leadership and purpose in a world that so craves it . . . even though it might not realise it. A war against complacency . . .'

'Uh . . . boss?' dared Maurice.

PT swung round to face him and yelled, 'FOR THE LAST TIME . . . !' and finally saw the scene unfolding on the screens.

'It seems we have company,' he said calmly. 'No matter. My lair is impregnable. Let them knock themselves out. We have more than enough time to finish what we're here for. Now where was I? Oh yes. Complacency.'

This time it was Sam Wheeler who dared to interrupt.

'*Nothing's* impregnable.'

'What?'

'There is *always* a chink. A loophole. A weak link.'

'My dear persistent hippie-haired boy. Allow me to explain. The only way someone can enter the lair of PT Cruiser is if they *are* PT Cruiser. Every electronic entry permission at MOTH is encrypted with my personal genetic code. So, unless by some dillion-to-one chance you share really big bits of my DNA, the chances of gaining entry here are less than zero. The House *always* wins.' And he smiled a nauseating smile. 'And, in this case, it's my house.'

There was silence for a moment. Then Buster Mustang spoke for the entire rest of the room.

'Wow. You really are a wally.'

'Am I indeed? Okay, Mr Mustang. Let me – as they say – *give you a break*. How would you like to have a go at removing that really big red plug, and shutting down the entire power of Xenon just before its global launch to an expectant world?'

Buster said nothing, but walked slowly over to the plug, leaned down and pulled. It didn't budge.

He pulled again. No dice.

'Ha! Do you think I'd leave the future of Xenon – and the subjugation of all mankind – to a big red plug that just anyone could pull out? Maurice, say, when he's doing the housework? Oh no. It's my Excalibur. My Sword in the Stone. And I am Arthur.'

'Umm . . . boss?'

'MAURICE! Don't make me send for Sergei. Piranhas aren't fussy in the dark . . .'

'BOSS, LOOK AT THE SCREEN! SHE'S GETTING IN!' blurted Maurice as fast as he could.

PT turned round a second time, and the remaining colour drained from his face.

The loophole. In person.

The screen showed a blonde girl in a designer camouflage jacket hold her palm up to the entry panel – and the door to the lair opening with a just-audible *szzzzzzjjoup*.

The room filled up with people, guns and, in one corner, massive relief.

PT Cruiser realised the enormity of his mistake. Project Daughter.

His own DNA had betrayed him.

'That's him,' said Cabriola Cruiser. 'In the –' she whispered the word as if she couldn't believe she was saying it – 'onesie.'

'You!' said PT Cruiser. 'A lifetime's work betrayed by my own flesh and blood.'

Cabriola turned away to avoid his gimlet gaze. 'I'm sorry,' she said simply.

And she caught the eye – just for an instant – of Sam Wheeler, who nodded to her in silent acknowledgement.

PT shook his head, staring at his errant daughter. 'Looking at you now,' he muttered, 'I wish I'd never played with that blasted test tube.'

A tall, distinguished-looking gentleman stepped forward.

'Mr Cruiser, I presume?' said the headmaster. 'I'm rather afraid it's game over.'

FORTY-FIFTH

In which it all comes to an end

In less than a second, the word's greatest computer genius and his remaining henchmen were surrounded by real-life commandos.

At their head, Cabriola Cruiser quickly scanned the room then headed straight towards to the big red Xenon plug, and leaned down.

'Noooooo!' wailed the demonic inventor. 'DON'T DO THAT! The world *wants* Xenon. It *needs* Xenon. People don't want to stress and strive and fail anymore. They *want* to be controlled. Can't you see? Xenon is where happiness lives.'

But Cabriola wasn't listening. And PT watched, helpless, as his only child leaned down and pulled out the plug that detached the Xenon superbrain from the innermost thoughts and fears of everyone who'd ever played it.

'Right!' said the nutty dillionaire to his only daughter, clearly very cross. 'You are *so* grounded.'

Across Bunsfold, people woke up from a dream they hadn't realised they'd been having. Lines of traffic finally started moving as the workmen with the STOP/GO signs remembered where they were. In the backs of cars, teenagers dropped their screens and started looking out of the window again. Sam Wheeler's dad put down his Xenon console, walked downstairs and made an omelette.

They were all waking from the strangest nightmare.

Just as one mean man saw his dastardly dream dissolve into dust.

PT Cruiser surveyed the scene in the lair for the last time. To his left, a throbbing machine that, despite the crowd of homeland security professionals and the bristling firearms, still managed to exude a powerful sense of impending menace. The hallmark of *really* good design.

To his right, a helmeted racing driver, arms folded, standing there staring into it. Or so PT assumed. Hard to tell with a dark visor.

'Before I depart to face my fate,' he said to the headmaster, 'a fate you no doubt believe I richly deserve, may I address my nemesis?'

The headmaster nodded.

'Mr The Stig,' he began, 'we are not so different, you and I. We both –'

'Uh, boss?' coughed Maurice, from between two burly officers.

'RIGHT, that's IT!' exploded the dillionaire genius. 'SERGEI!'

Meanwhile, Sam Wheeler found himself listening to a chorus of spontaneous whoops, shouts, cheers and even occasional cries of anguish. And they were all coming from him.

As they walked out into the fresh air of the MOTH courtyard, Ford, Minnie and Buster were going mad as well. Call it elation, call it relief, but they hugged and laughed and cried like . . . well, like kids who'd just saved the world.

And the sun had come out at last.

The Head walked over and shook each of their hands in turn.

'What you've all achieved was quite . . . well, for once I'm lost for words. I'm really very proud of you.'

They all fell silent for a second, as the same blush took hold of all of them except Minnie, who didn't blush easily.

'Hey, you too, cellmate,' said Buster, who thought about hugging his distinguished-looking friend, but then didn't because, well, nobody hugs headmasters.

And then the four kids started whooping and hugging again.

It was Ford who finally broke off, and turned back to the Head.

'Sir, looking up at those thirty-two screens and seeing you and an entire police force arriving was the single greatest moment of my life. How did you get back up here so fast?'

'Stroke of luck, Mr Harrison. When I ran back through the courtyard after leaving you and Buster, I discovered they'd left a helicopter gunship on the front drive with the keys in. I've a bit of flying time from my stint in the navy and, well, Bob's your uncle.'

Ford smiled to himself. First because he was happy, and secondly because, well, Bob was indeed his uncle.

Minnie finally broke off from hugging the boys and looked back towards the lair. 'Where's The Stig?' she said. 'And *phwooar*, isn't he *buff*, by the way?'

'Not especially,' said Ford rather quickly.

'I think he's still in the lair,' said Buster, 'staring at that giant engine.'

'Perhaps they're related,' said Sam, and everybody laughed. 'Well, I think we need to go back and thank him. I mean, that bloke really came through for us.'

Then Sam led the way back towards the chamber, past policemen who were busy cordoning things off, as they do.

When they arrived at the lair, The Stig was still standing like a statue opposite the giant engine.

They stood behind him, not knowing quite what to say, and then the headmaster called out to them through the buggy-shaped hole in the wall.

'Sorry to interrupt, everybody, but I have a rather heroic friend here to see you.'

He was holding a lead. And on the end of it was a limping, scarred but tail-wagging scruffy mongrel called TG.

The children ran up and mobbed her. TG wriggled so hard with excitement that it looked as if her tail would fall off.

'Here's the REAL hero of the story,' said Sam, grabbing and hugging her with tears in his eyes.

And, just for a second, everything in the world seemed

perfect. But only for a second.

Because just then, and quite suddenly, TG Dog stiffened, and started to growl. A low, determined growl that Buster and Sam knew meant something was very wrong.

Now her teeth were bared, and she was shaking and barking desperately.

'What's *wrong*, girl?' said Buster. The children pulled away from her in fright, and the Head struggled to hold on to the lead.

With a shock, Sam saw that TG seemed to be barking at . . . *Minnie?*

'Hey, calm down, TG. It's only the Cooper,' he said, nonplussed. 'She's one of us . . .'

Minnie smiled and walked towards TG, her arms outstretched. 'Oh, for goodness' sake, come here, you silly dog. I'm not *that* bad . . .'

And she leaned down to hug the madly barking mongrel.

But she didn't hug it.

Her left arm shot out at extraordinary speed, and grabbed TG by the throat.

'I'm worse.'

Then, in one lightning and sickeningly violent movement, she yanked the scruffy hound clear off the ground and rammed her head back against the wall of the lair.

'Told you dogs don't like me,' she said. She turned to the boys, smiling strangely.

'And I don't like dogs.'

And the girl they had known as their best friend began to change before their eyes.

The bright, expressive eyes started to lose their expression and change shape – then melted like a waxwork placed too close to a fire. The flesh peeled away and morphed into a harder, shinier, much darker surface. Where the eyes had been, red lights appeared: dim at first, but coming into focus as they spelled out a series of words.

STIG . . . DESTRUCTION . . . IMMINENT . . .

Ford reeled backwards. 'No . . . NO! You? It can't be . . . Minnie . . . you're *the Deathbot*?'

And in that split second – that sickening, indescribably evil split second, the terrible truth dawned on them all.

Minnie Cooper was the Deathbot. And she'd been the Deathbot all along.

A second message in red lights.

EAT . . . DOG . . . FIRST . . .

A mouth appeared where a mouth would be. It opened to reveal two fangs. NO, thought Buster Mustang. Not again!

He flew towards her. Her arm shot out – faster than a human eye could register – and swatted him away like a baseball.

HAVE A NICE DAY, VIRGIL.

Then the robotic figure of the Deathbot – now part Minnie Cooper, part killer drone robot – made as if to bite the stomach of TG Dog.

The second it did, the mysterious white-suited racing driver people call The Stig finally spun away from the Chamber of

Combustion, and raced towards her.

The creature dropped the dog and faced its mission. The digits flashed again – **DO . . . YOU . . . FEEL . . . LUCKY . . . STIG?** – just as the one voice on the planet that could possibly get the killer robot's attention called out to it from immediately behind.

'Deathbot!' cried PT Cruiser. 'Can we talk about this?'

The creature turned its head round, slowly, to face its creator. *All the way* round. Those last ninety degrees were properly creepy.

PT went on. 'Mission Override XYYZZZ88. Abort destruction of Stig.'

The robot hesitated for a second. Then, **SORRY, DAD. NO CAN DO.**

PT Cruiser looked angry. 'What *is it* with me and daughters?'

Just then, a heavily armed SWAT team jumped through the hole in the wall and took up station directly opposite the killer robot.

The strange metal head – still weirdly bearing some of the features of the girl they knew as Minnie Cooper – swivelled to face them.

The creature flashed a message on the visor.

COME . . . ON . . . THEN . . . ! YOU . . . WANT . . . SOME . . . ? YOU . . . WANT . . . SOME . . . I'LL . . . GIVE . . . IT . . . YOU. I'LL . . . TAKE . . . YOU . . . ALL . . . ON.

In desperation, PT tried a different tack.

'That's hardly necessary, Deathbot,' he said in a placating voice. 'Yes, I *know* I programmed you to grab Mr The Stig and jump into the Chamber of Combustion to your mutually assured destruction . . .'

He looked sideways sheepishly at The Stig, and indeed the SWAT team.

'But now I've met my nemesis, face to helmet, he's not half as terrible as I thought. You build these things up, they fester – when all the time what was needed was a little clearing of the air. And now we've had the time to chat and hang out together, I'm certain things will be different. So, Mr The Stig, what do you say? Friends?'

Unsurprisingly, The Stig didn't reply. So PT turned to his indescribably evil drone instead.

'Deathbot? Hello? Are either of you two even *listening* to me?'

The answer to that question was 'no'.

Because, unbeknownst to PT Cruiser, the Deathbot was now beyond the reach or reason of anyone, including him. Beyond, even, the reach of Mission Override XYYZZZ88. Having spent its entire existence hunting one prey, it had become infected with the same, fatal obsession that afflicted the man who'd created it.

As it gazed into the impenetrable dark visor of **TARGET STIG**. it knew that here, finally, was a prey that would remain forever immune to its terror.

So it did the only thing of which it was capable. It shot out two Narnium arms and grabbed The Stig to its chest. Then, feet hovering just off the ground, it accelerated towards the throbbing Chamber of Combustion.

The air was filled with the sound of an enormous induction roar, like a canyon drawing its last breath. The massive piston, the width of a moon rocket, plummeted like a discarded Saturn V, then thrust upwards towards the spark that gave it life.

And then, with the implacable logic of a machine that has out-evolved its creator, the robot finally fulfilled its single purpose by hurling itself and The Stig into the Engine of Doom – just as the piston smashed into the roof of the chamber.

Everyone present took what felt like the same shocked breath. The piston fell. On its top surface were the crushed, flat, black remains of 'Minnie Cooper' – in reality a Stigicidal cyborg in a tartan skirt, some threads of which still clung to the wreckage. And next to it . . . was that a smidge of white? Tricky to tell; it moved downwards so fast.

All they knew was that there was nothing solid left inside.

A crack of thunder ricocheted around them, the loudest anyone present had ever heard. A subterranean rumbling.

Then nothing.

Finally, Ford Harrison spoke.

'Oh no,' he said. 'They've killed The Stig.'

EPILOGUE

Three months later

It was a beautiful autumnal Sunday afternoon in sleepy Bunsfold.

And Sam Wheeler was happy.

He rode his BMX across the sandy recreation ground, now teeming with kids playing football while parents watched, walked dogs, held hands, argued and worried about what colour to paint the front door. The normal stuff of normal lives. Where happiness lives. Alongside sadness, pasta, love, mud, friendship, exams and yoghurt.

A few large houses still lined the hill that led away from the centre. And way up on its own, the largest mansion of all still glowered over the town like an abandoned asylum where some crazy dillionaire woulda got away with it too, if not for some pesky kids.

And a pesky dog, thought Sam, dismounting and hugging the excited scruffy mongrel that bounded up to him.

'She's looking fit,' he called to the two kids approaching on their own bikes. 'You too, Fordo. And smelling slightly less like a sewer today. That's good.'

TG rolled over, begging for a tummy tickle. Sam obliged.

It was a fantastic afternoon, and no one felt like going to the Den just yet.

'Race you round the town!' said Ford. 'Catch me if you can, losers!' And he set off at his usual sedate pace and in a riding style strongly reminiscent of Mary Poppins.

Sam thought he'd seen faster-accelerating goalposts.

As Ford led them in a low-speed chase round Bunsfold, TG Dog bounded along beside, panting like a dog living a dog's life to the full.

Right up to the locked gates of Bunsfold High, where they all stopped to catch their breath.

Schools on a Saturday always have a left-behind feeling. Sam cast his mind back to the first day, and the hay, and the charming Cruiser Crew. It all seemed a long, long time ago.

He looked up at the cockerel weather vane, still with an LA Dodgers baseball cap perched on its head.

Only now it was on back to front.

He looked back over at Buster Mustang, and grinned.

'One day you're going to have to tell me how you do that,' he said.

'Sure,' said the American boy. 'One day.'

They rested in the sunshine, leaning on their handlebars and swigging ginger beers in a comfortable silence.

'You know,' said Sam, 'I should have guessed something was up when Minnie read "LA Dodgers" from right down here.'

'We all should have. But she was . . . lovely,' said Ford. 'And we wanted her to be true.'

'If a bit shorter,' said Sam with a wink.

'What can I say?' said Ford, with a shrug. 'I fancied a tall killer robot.'

'Hey . . . don't worry about it,' said Buster Mustang. 'It's the oldest story in the world. Boy meets girl. Boy falls in love. Boy discovers girl is evil killer robot. Boy sees girl crushed in giant Chamber of Combustion.' And he paused to flip his bike into an expert wheelie. 'Happens all the time.'

'You know the weirdest thing of all?' said Ford. 'I miss her.'

'The Cooper? Oh yeah, me too,' said Sam.

And they each held their ginger-beer bottles in the air, in a toast.

'To Minnie Cooper,' said Buster.

'To Minnie Cooper,' said Ford.

'Grrrrrrrrrrrr,' growled TG Dog, who evidently wasn't missing her at all.

Then the scruffy animal grew tired of all the chat, and resumed the important task of sniffing along the school fence for any signs of smarty-pants foxes. Always so *full of themselves*.

Sam broke the silence.

'I hear Spooner's taking something positive from the whole experience,' he said. 'He's biting a rook.'

'I heard that too,' laughed Ford. 'It's a proper toe-and-shell, apparently.'

And they fell about. Then, when the ginger beers were finished, they set off for the Swiss-roll-shaped hump in the woods they knew as BCHQ.

When they arrived, a familiar figure was sitting on top of the Reliant Robin. A figure they hadn't seen for months.

A blonde girl with long hair and a denim jacket sat on the upturned car, one long leg hanging down the side like a leopard's tail. A normal-looking BMX was propped up nearby.

'Blimey,' said Sam. 'Cabriola Cruiser, I presume.'

'Hello, new kid,' said the girl.

Another silence. Less comfortable.

'So when did you get back?' asked Ford.

'Oh, this morning,' said the girl. 'They kept me up there for weeks for questioning. Then, when Dad was finally put away, they sent me back.'

'So – are you here for good now?' said Ford.

'Yup,' said Cabriola. 'They've appointed Maurice Marina as my legal guardian.'

'Hmm. Interesting role model,' said Buster.

'How's your dad?' asked Sam.

'Hasn't said a word since it all happened,' said Cabriola. 'Just sits in his cell drawing big white helmets on the wall.' She blinked hard, took a deep breath and looked into the distance. 'Not sure why I visit.'

'Wow,' said Sam. 'He was really hung up on The Stig, wasn't he? A proper hopeless man-crush.'

'And he wasn't even all that buff,' said Ford rather too quickly.

'The Stig? Oh no, I completely disagree. I thought he was really handsome actually,' said Cabriola.

'Whaaaat?' said Ford. 'He wore a *helmet* all the time, for heaven's sake . . .'

Buster Mustang interrupted him. 'Will they send PT back to California now?'

'Shouldn't think so,' said the girl. 'He's never been to California.'

'Wait a minute . . . so where *is* he from, really?'

Cabriola bit her lip. 'Eccles.'

'Ha!' said Buster. 'I knew it. I never could place his accent.'

Sam let out a long, low whistle. 'Wow. Well, that's a turn-up.'

'I think he thought no one would take a tech dillionaire from Eccles very seriously,' said Cabriola.

'So why are you here?' said Ford. 'What can *we* do for you?'

'Word on the street is your gang's short by one girl these days,' said Cabriola. 'After what happened to Minnie Cooper . . .'

'Grrrrrrrrr,' interrupted TG.

'. . . so I thought I'd apply for the vacancy.'

And she looked sideways, away from their surprised faces.

Buster, Ford and TG Dog looked taken aback. Then extremely dubious.

Sam didn't.

'Absolutely!' He beamed instantly. 'Consider yourself hired!' And he high-fived her. 'What you did at the race . . . that took guts. That really, really took guts.'

He looked at Buster, and then at Ford, and nodded at them to do the same.

And – eventually – the two of them shuffled up and high-fived her too.

Sam looked reproachfully at TG, who reluctantly shuffled forward and offered her a front leg to shake.

It was the last paw.

'So,' said Sam, 'that's settled then. Now I think it's time for . . . a race.'

Taking her cue, Cabriola slid down from the Reliant's bonnet and mounted her BMX in one strangely feline movement.

Sam grinned. 'A race to . . .'

The others hunched on their saddles, ready to go. TG Dog crouched alongside, ready to go.

'The river!' called Sam.

Three boys, one girl and a dog sped away laughing together, across the rec and towards Bunsfold Bridge.

When they got there, Sam Wheeler gazed at the bank on the other side. 'Reckon we could jump it?' he asked.

'Nah,' said Ford.

'Marginal,' said Cabriola.

'Easy,' said Buster Mustang. The others turned to look at him quizzically. 'All you need is an evil killer robot chasing your ass . . .'

'Hmm,' said Sam. 'Well, only one way to find out.'

The four of them retreated and then turned to take up formation, facing the river. And after a 'Three, two, one . . . GO!' from Sam they hurtled towards the water and launched their bikes as one towards the opposite bank.

Three kids and a dog made it. One rather shorter boy, not so much.

When they'd fished out Ford and towelled him down with their T-shirts, the five friends sat together on the grass in silence.

'So the gang is complete,' said Sam. 'All we need now is a new adventure.'

And just then something really quite strange happened.

In the distance, a middle-aged man they'd never seen before walked straight out of Bunsfold Forest and across the field towards them.

He was wearing a white lab coat. And in his left hand he carried a single white envelope.

The gang were all too startled to say anything.

The man walked right up to Sam and handed him the letter.

Then, without a word, he turned and walked straight back into the forest.

'Blimey,' said Sam. 'Well, that came out of nowhere.'

They looked at the envelope. It read:

TO: THE TOP GEAR GANG
FROM: THE PRODUCER
SUBJECT: YOUR NEXT CHALLENGE

They all gathered around as Sam opened it.

All, that is, except TG Dog, who took several steps away towards the fields, ears pricked.

In the distance, far, far away, she saw a murder of crows rise as one and wheel away in a strange formation.

Then she caught, too far away for human ears to hear, the faintest sound of rusty bagpipes on the breeze.

She wagged her tail just once, before bounding back to join her gang.

The Top Gear Gang.

TO BE CONTINUED . . .

COMING SOON

ARE YOU READY TO RACE?

BBC TopGear

100 120
80 140

THE STIG

DRIVES AGAIN

JON CLAYDON & TIM LAWLER

Piccadilly
PRESS

Piccadilly
P R E S S

Thank you for choosing a Piccadilly Press book.

If you would like to know more about our authors, our books or if you'd just like to know what we're up to, you can find us online.

www.piccadillypress.co.uk

You can also find us on:

We hope to see you soon!